BUILD

UNIVER

William A. Pollard

INSIDE

© 2024 **Europe Books**| London
www.europebooks.co.uk | info@europebooks.co.uk

ISBN 9791220153065
First edition: September 2024

INSIDE

BOOKS BY THE AUTHOR

MY ROGUE GENE
ISBN : 978-1-80074-296-3

Bill's autobiography. Full of amusing anecdotes from his past, from the time he was born up to the time he left the army after twelve years service.

Olympia Publishers
Amazon Bookstore

MY GROWN-UP ROGUE GENE
ISBN: 978-1-80439-313-0

More nonsense from Bill's rogue gene, now grown-up and still interfering with Bill's life.
This is a sequel to *My Rogue Gene*, highlighting Bill's life from the time he left the army to his life in civvy street and into retirement.

Olympia Publishers
Amazon Bookstore

BEHIND ROSE BORDERED WINDOWS
(Winner of the Golden Book Prize at the Rome Literary Awards, March 2024)
ISBN - 979-1-22014-338-7

William Colbert's wife dies. Everyone is convinced her death was an accident, including William. He has inherited a country manor in a remote part of the country, but his new life is thrown into disarray when he witnesses distressing events through the windows of the five picture postcard cottages facing his new home... Nobody believes what he has seen, until the truth about his inheritance, and his wife, is revealed.

Europe Books
Amazon Bookstore

LUCKY, OR WHAT...?
ISBN: 979-1-22014-866-5

How many people, do you think, have just wished that they had more good luck in their lives? What you don't realise is that the quicker you use up your good luck, the nearer you are to having a shed load of bad luck.
Playing an on-line game, eight finalists don't know that if they lose the game, they die. Something else they don't know is that if they win the game, they die.
Either way, they're dead...

Europe Books
Amazon Bookstore

ACKNOWLEDGEMENT

My thanks to Marie Brewer.

Marie read, then re-read, then read again, my manuscript for this book to wheedle out my stupid errors and omissions. Without her, I wouldn't have been able to put together a relevant storyline.

Table of Contents

THE CAST
(in order of appearance)

OUTSIDE

Sidney (Sid) Smethers	Himself. Born 1987
Sara Smethers	Sid's wife. Born 1987
Suzy Summers, nee Smethers	Sid's daughter. Born 2008. Married to Sonny
Stan	Suzy's ex-boyfriend from her schooldays
Steve and Stella	Stan's parents
Spencer	Sara's ex-boyfriend from her schooldays
Sid's dentist	He's got a pearly white smile, with perfect teeth
Sahila	Tangiers hotel receptionist. A greedy bloke
Siham	Tangiers hotel chef. Can be bribed
Saloua	Tangiers doctor
Seth	Sid's neighbour
Scott Smethers	Sid's brother

Symone Smethers	Scott's wife
Sean	Symone's father
Sandra	Spencer's wife
Pub landlord	Himself. Sean did a good deal with him for Symone's wedding reception
Sergio and Sage	Sid's Italy holiday acquaintances
Salvatore	The Italy hotel's manager
Sabine	The Italy hotel's receptionist
Severo	Italy's search and rescue organiser
Hospital nurse	Herself
Shane	Sid's personal trainer
Sonny Summers	Suzy's husband
Sunny Summers	Suzy's daughter

INSIDE

Brian, the brain manager	aka the C.O. (Commanding Officer)
Lee, the lookout manager	aka the Eyes - not to be confused with Lee, the listening manager
Piers, the pump manager	aka the Heart
Lee, the listening manager	aka the Ears - not to be confused with Lee, the lookout manager
Merv, the message wires & ideas chip manager	aka the Nerves
Mick, the masher	aka Mastication
Fred, the food shoveller	aka the Throat - shovels food into the chute
Kevin, the kitchen manager	aka the Stomach
Waste chute	aka the Intestines - there's a manhole at the top sealing the chute from the kitchen
Tim, the trapdoor manager	aka the Anal Sphincter
Wally, the wax manager	aka Ear wax

Daphne, the defence force manager	aka the Immune system
Ida	Daphne's assistant
Billy, The big wrapping manager	aka the Skin
Bella, the bellows manager	aka the Lungs - she is loud and pumps iron
Manny, the metabolism status manager	aka the Liver - married to Fay
Fay, the filters manager	aka the Kidneys - married to Manny
Max, the mechanics manager	aka the Skeleton
Connor, the courier and keep fit manager	Brian's runner
Tommy, the temperature manager	Speaks for itself
Nick, the nourishment manager	aka the Blood supply
Theola, the thermoregulators manager	aka the sweat glands
Tony, the tank manager	aka the Bladder
Sienna, the sniffer & smell manager	aka the Nose

Reproduction Departments Inside

SID:

Axel, the aquarium manager   aka the Prostate

Blaire, the ballbag manager   aka the Testes

Edgar, the Epididymis manager   Responsible for categorisation & measuring of Sid's tadpoles (aka Sperm)

Eddie, the exit chute manager   aka the Vas Deferens & Urethra (Penis)

SARA:

Elsie, the egg production manager   aka ovaries

Anita, the arrival lounge manager   aka the oviduct & fallopian tubes

Eva, the egg hotel manager   aka Uterus

Prologue

Look in a mirror. What do you see?

Okay, I know that you see *you*, but look closer. Look into your eyes. Look up your nose. Look into your mouth.

Still can't see any more than anyone else? That's understandable. You see your eyes, and ears, and nose, and mouth and throat and stomach, and lots of other appendages that you ignore until one of them gets sick- then you ask yourself, "What's going on inside my body?"

You might just have an innocent hang-over from last night's partying. Perhaps you're battling through something more troubling, like a vicious bout of the Tangier Trots, brought on by something you munched during last night's partying.

Whatever it is that made you wonder what goes on inside you, let me dispel any ideas you may have that your bodily functions are being controlled by some biological, chemical, anatomical or physical reaction.

Doctors spend many years studying and remembering the size, shape, location, orientation and function of every organ closely packed inside your skeletal frame and conveniently covered by a waterproof coating we call our skin. Those years are also spent studying other, more noticeable stuff; your nails and hair and fingers and arms and legs and toes and feet and lots of other attachments that all require care and attention to keep them in tip-top condition. Even more years are taken up learning how to repair your body, both inside and out, when something goes wrong with it.

The truth is, your anatomy and physiology is far more interesting than you think.

The doctors and nurses have all learned their stuff from books with intricate pictures of your insides, showing where your heart and your kidneys and your intestines and your lungs and your stomach and your brain, and everything else, is located. They learn what they look like and what all these organs and bones and joints do to keep you upright.

Complex, eh? Not really, because what the doctors and nurses learn from books and lectures and endless homework sessions long into the night is only half right!

It's true...

"Why?" I hear you ask.

Well, what you don't realise is that there is a whole community of tiny workers managing your bodily functions. A really, really tiny community of people with the singular purpose of keeping your anatomy and physiology working in first class condition. They rarely go on strike for more pay because they don't get paid. They don't need money or credit cards or bank accounts, because they have everything they need inside you. They have food and somewhere to sleep and regular changes of clothes. So, for them, what's the point of having money? No point at all. An absolutely useless commodity. They're happy as they are... Until something goes wrong.

Okay, you still have kidneys, and a brain, and lungs, and a bladder and everything else that doctors and nurses learn about from their books, but I can assure you that a miniscule community of people are managing those anatomical assets. They shovel and pump and inflate and mix and clean and dispose of the rubbish - just like a colony of ants in their nest. A busy factory. Everything

20

the same as what we, as grown-up humans, do. They watch where you're going to make sure you don't bump into things and they hear the noises that are being made outside their environment. But this colony never leaves its nest. The community is inside you for life. You were born with it and it grows with you.

Still not convinced?

Okay, read on and you will be persuaded.

Chapter 1
(Average Sid)

Before I delve deep inside your body, just remember one thing… All your organs are dependent on each other. If one system goes down you can bet your big toe that others will follow pretty quickly, unless you can help your inside community put right that which is wrong. Okay?

Okay.

I suppose that the logical place to start is with your brain.

Yes, you do have a brain, although I know one or two blokes whose brains consist of just two brain cells. As long as there is a spark between those two brain cells those blokes seem to function normally, but it doesn't take much for them to adopt a tangential path away from normality - usually a few pints of beer…

Anyway, back to your brain.

Your brain detects and processes sensory information, activating bodily responses. Simply put, the brain regulates whole-body physiology, functions and movements. Your very own internal computer.

This is an important job, yes? So it is labour intensive. With millions of miles of wiring (you call this wiring your nerves), regulation of body movements, muscle control and lots of other functions to manage, you cannot survive without your brain unless, of course, you are in the two brain cell league of idiots previously mentioned.

Brian, the brain manager, knows this and he has a staff of forty or fifty tiny operatives sat in front of their PC consoles, busily tapping away on their keyboards to control all the anatomical and physiological functions of your body. They continually monitor the thirty computer servers that communicate with the other departments inside you.

*

Outside, Sidney Smethers - Sid to his mates - is an average type of guy. He is the subject of my exploration of your insides.

Everything about him is average. He got average marks from the exams he took during an average education. He's got average intelligence, and an average height and weight - and an average physique. He has average eyesight and he is far from handsome because he has an average face, with average features and average ears protruding from his average sized head. During PT, at school, he was always chosen in the middle of the choosing sessions. Never first choice because he wasn't good enough, but then, never last choice because he was better than the losers. Just average at sport. His style of clothes is average. Not loud and colourful but, again, not plain and boring. Just average.

Sid is so average he is almost invisible. In fact, so invisible that you might miss him if he was standing on a box and waving at you with a big flag from the middle of a field, even though he is the only person in that field.

Like I said - an average type of guy.

He lives in an average semi-detached house situated on an average estate with his wife Sara.

Now, Sara is far from average.

She is gorgeous. She has a gorgeous figure that is coveted by almost every woman she meets. She's got a film-star face, she spends a lot of time making her gorgeous hair just right to please Sid, and she wears clothes that complement her bright, sunny, outgoing personality.

Sid is the envy of all his friends and acquaintances because Sara is so gorgeous. There isn't any one of Sid's mates who wouldn't swap their present wife for Sara. Quite what she saw in Sid when they first met is anybody's guess, but they both worship each other and neither would let anything come between them.

Anyway, we're going to look at Sid's community of really, really tiny people.

It is tea time at Sid's House and he has decided to give his beautiful Sara a night off, from cooking, by getting a take-away meal from his local Chinese take-away shop. He returned home with two plastic bags containing trays of pre-cooked roasted duck breast with ginger sauce, egg fried rice, chow mein, aromatic king prawn stir fry, pan fried scallops, six sticks of pork satay and two crunch spring rolls. For dessert he took home a bowl of sherry trifle and two large cream-filled eclairs.

For Sara, he got a couple of crispy pancakes with some egg fried rice and a small yogurt...

Watching Sid tuck into his take-away, Sara decided to remind him about the folly of gorging on so much high cholesterol stuff. She never nags Sid, but sometimes he just needs a gentle reminder that his present healthy condition will not last forever.

"You do realise that you're going to have a heart attack after eating all that fatty food, don't you?"

"Nah. This is just a snack," smiled Sid.

"Okay, have it your way," she sighed. "I hope you're not expecting me to visit you in hospital with tubes entering every orifice you have. You know I don't like hospitals."

"I won't be going to hospital soon," he replied, trying to appease Sara's concern, at the same time stuffing a King Prawn into his mouth.

"Can I have that in writing?" she asked. "Talking of which, have you renewed your life insurance policy? I'm going to need some help paying off the mortgage."

"Don't worry," Sid smiled. "I've got a few years in me before you'll need that."

I wonder if Sid knew what was actually going on inside…

Chapter 2
(Incoming…!)

Most people ignore their eyes… Until they get something in one of them. This could be a fleck of mascara, or an eye lash, or some dust, or somebody's angry finger.

Believe it, or not, your eyes are not as incredibly complex as the professionals would like you to think. They will try to persuade you that there is stuff called Vitreous Humour, and Macula, and Choroid, and Retina, and all sorts of other stuff inside your eyes that merit long passages and colourful pictures in textbooks. Not so…

Inside Sid, Lee, the lookout manager - not to be confused with Lee, the listening manager - sits in front of a PC console that is attached to a pair of huge binoculars inside each one of Sid's eyeballs. From here he controls the direction and focus of both of Sid's eyes. From his lookout station Lee keeps watch on where Sid is going, and what his hands and feet are doing, and what other people are doing, and how far away that lamp post is, and where the puddles of water are and how incredibly fast that bus is travelling towards him as he crosses the road. In fact, anything that is likely to have any kind of effect on Sid's forward facing, vertical status. From Sid's perspective, vertical is good. Unless, that is, he is on the cusp of falling asleep or he can feel Sara's roving hand interrupting his thoughts of tomorrow's breakfast as he slides into dreamland...

Lee transmits his observation status to Brian, the brain manager, to enable Brian to make the important decisions about Sid's movements, and he also copies the data to other parts of Sid's body to keep the managers of those parts updated on events appertaining to Sid's environment.

When Sid poured the contents of the take-away trays onto a plate for his tea Lee sat up, his eyes wide at the enormity of Sid's meal.

Hurriedly picking up his microphone he made an emergency announcement over the Tannoy system to all departments.

"This is an emergency announcement to all departments. INCOMING! All departments prepare for an excessive input of nourishment…"

Piers, the pump (aka heart) manager, opened the taps on the barrels of Adrenalin, kept in the Adrenal store for such events, to regulate Sid's cardiac output. He worried that he may not have a sufficient supply of Adrenalin to activate an anticipated rapid acceleration of Sid's pump beat and maintain its speed, brought on by an overload of excessive nourishment…

*

Outside, Sid happily tucked into his feast, not knowing about the flurry of activity inside him as he chatted about nothing in particular to Sara.

One thing he did notice, however, was a slight increase in his heart rate as he munched through his enormous meal. Bump, bump, bump, bump, Sid's heart banged against his ribs in protest at the extra work Piers, the pump manager, had made it do. Sid thought nothing of the increased work that Piers had initiated…

Suzy, Sid's daughter, is a precocious young girl. We'll come back to Suzy much later, when she gets a blackhead, but she gets her good looks and intelligence from Sara and she is able to wrap Sid around her little finger any time she likes.

"Mum?"

"Yes, pet?" answered Sara.

"Can I stay over at Stan's house tonight?"

"Why?"

Now, Sara knows precisely why Suzy wants to stay over at Stan's house tonight. Suzy is, after all, a 'woman of the world', as she likes to think of herself, even though she has never been any further than Margate. Sara knows that Steve and Stella, Stan's parents, are away on a long weekend in some far off balmy climate, sipping fluorescent looking drinks while they sat at a bar on the beach - and Stan will be on his own while they are away. Sara is also aware of what teenagers do when their parents can't see what they are up to. Parents are always keen to interrupt any 'goings on' that should not be going on, aren't they? Sara remembered that she was once a young sixteen year old herself, and she had some good memories of Spencer, a class friend from her own schooldays, and herself rolling about in a hay barn. Sid doesn't know about Spencer 'cos he's never asked.

Suzy thought up a good reason.

"Well, we've got a lot of homework tonight and I don't think you would like me to walk home when it's late, would you?"

"No, that's true. I can come and pick you up when you're ready."

There was a pause for some more thought from Suzy, during which Sara thought to herself '*Homework, my arse. The only homework they'll be doing is playing mummies and daddies…*'

Suzy proffered a contrived response. "I'm sure you won't want to be disturbed from your film tonight. Can I, Mum? Can I?"

"I don't know, Suzy. I'll think about it."

"Oh, mum. It'll be too late, soon. There'll be no point in going and I won't get a good mark for my homework if Stan doesn't help me."

Then Suzy had a flash of inspiration.

"Anyway, this homework is a joint project so I won't be able to finish it without Stan 'cos he's the partner chosen for me by my teacher. Can I?"

Turning to Sid, Suzy pleaded, "Can I, Dad? Can I?. Pleeeeease."

Sid had been listening to this conversation…

Chapter 3
(A rock and a hard place)

You'll never believe this, but you don't actually have what the professionals call a Tympanic Membrane.

There are microphones attached to stands that are bolted to the floor of your ear canals, in front of walls dividing your ear canals from what the doctors call Eustachian Tubes.

Actually, there is a long flight of stairs inside each of the Eustachian Tubes leading down to your Nasopharynx, an area between the base of your skull and the soft palate at the back of your throat. Sitting on top of the soft palate, within the Nasopharynx chamber, is a platform that connects each of the staircases in the Eustachian Tubes leading up to your ears.

Inside, Lee, the listening manager (not to be confused with Lee, the lookout manager) sits in an office located in an area right at the top of one of your Eustachian Tubes. This is where the professionals think your Malleus, Incus and Stapes are located. It's also an office. From this office Lee monitors all the sounds picked up by the microphones attached to the stands that are bolted to the floor of your ear canals.

The sounds are then digitally transmitted from Lee's PC to Brian's terminal. Brian is, we should all by now know, the brain manager. I reckon Lee and Brian have got something secretive going on between them. Lee has been seen furtively lurking around the platform in the Nasopharynx chamber, as if she is waiting for someone. More than just a tete-a-tete, I would say, but I can neither confirm nor deny that because they have never been seen together.

Anyway, Lee has just picked up on a conversation between Suzy and her mother about Suzy wanting to stay over at Stan's place.

*

Outside, Sid tried not to intrude in Sara and Suzy's conversation as he munched his way through his meal, but Suzy gave him no choice.

"Can I, Dad? Can I?. Pleeeeease."

That particular look on Suzy's face is usually too much for Sid to ignore. Suzy stares at him with puppy-dog eyes that would melt the heart of the most hardened serial murderer and she smiles the sweetest, most endearing smile that could easily be confused with the genuine and gentlest of smiles from an innocent Nun who has just received a massive donation from you.

This look always puts Sid between a rock and a hard place. A sideways glance from Sid to Sara confirmed that he had better not agree to this proposal - but neither did he want to upset the apple of his eye.

*

Back inside, Lee, listening manager, quickly typed out an urgent message to Brian:

> *URGENT MEMO*
> *From: Lee in listening*
> *To: Brian in brain*
> This message was sent with High importance
>
> *Urgent!*
>
> *Sid is being manipulated by Suzy... Again!*

*Suzy wants to sleep over at Stan's place but Sara
is not in favour of this proposal. You'd better
think of some way to get Sid out of this, or there
will be Hell to pay if he agrees.*

Lee.

Stabbing the send key on her terminal, Lee sat back
and hoped that she had not been too late to warn Brian.

Not so. At light speed, the message arrived on
Brian's screen almost immediately Suzy finished making
the request. Brian gave urgent instructions to Merv, the
message wires manager, to send a spark of inspiration to
Sid's ideas chip to give Sid a way out of the hole that
Suzy had dug for him.

The spark in Sid's ideas chip fired.

*

Outside, Sid suddenly thought up a solution to his 'rock
and a hard place' conundrum.

"Tell you what, my love, how about I pick up Stan
after tea, bring him here, and you can both do your
homework in my study? I'll take him home when you've
finished your project."

Now this remedy hit Suzy like a runaway bus. It
wasn't what she expected. Sid usually caved in to her
charms at times like this and it certainly was not the
response she wanted.

With a sigh and a somewhat sour look at Sara she
acquiesced.

"Okay. Thanks Daddy."

Sid was sure he detected a hint of sarcasm in the
'Thanks...' part of Suzy's response, but another glance at

Sara confirmed that he would not need to read his book in bed tonight. He wouldn't be able to if the look on Sara's face was anything to go by…

Conundrum over, Sid attacked his pan-fried Scallops.

*

Inside, Lee in listening breathed a sigh of relief that she had averted a possible disaster in Sid's life, but she couldn't shake that feeling of impending doom that always seems to descend upon her when something bad is about to happen.

Piers, the pump (aka Heart) manager, was a little concerned about Sid's slightly irregular pump beat. Perhaps he should look into this, sometime…

Chapter 4
(Excessive input of nourishment)

I bet you don't know that you've got some triplets inside you.

Yep. Three really, really tiny people, all brothers born on the same day within minutes of each other at the same time as Sid was born. These guys manage what is referred to as your Gastrointestinal Tract.

A big phrase, that, but don't panic. I'll explain what it is for you right now. Sit back and learn...

The Gastrointestinal Tract is just a posh word made up by some long dead anatomy boffin who liked to give simple things, like 'food passage', big words. Let's start at the top.

You cram your nourishment into a big hole in the front of your face. This hole is called the oral cavity, or mouth if you prefer the simpler version. This is the place where you masticate.

Now don't go getting hot under the collar. I know that word - masticate - sounds a bit lewd, but you are confusing it with an entirely different word with an entirely different meaning, requiring an entirely different activity... Settle down and pay attention!

Mastication is the action of chewing your food. You need to masticate so that the chunks of food that you shove into your oral cavity doesn't get stuck in your Gastrointestinal Tract and choke you.

Too technical? Okay, let's start again...

Mick, Fred and Kevin are triplets. They all work in harmony with each other to manage the nourishment that is forked into your mouth.

Mick, the masher, has the job of managing the mastication mechanism inside your mouth. This contraption shuts the hole in your face and then chews up, mashes, pummels, crushes and fragments the nourishment (aka food) you have just shoved in. The mastication plant requires a lot of maintenance by way of regular washing and scrubbing to clean out all the particles trapped in the teeth of the masticator. This exercise is carried out by Sid each night before he goes to bed - he brushes his teeth.

The next step in the process of providing nourishment for your body is implemented by Fred, the food shoveller.

Fred and his team gather all the masticated nourishment into a pile and they then shovel it onto a conveyor belt that carries it to the back of your mouth and tips it into what the professionals call the Oesophagus, another complicated word, but put simply - your throat.

In the outside world, your Oesophagus is approximately 25cm long, but in the inside world this pipe is really a very wide chute a few hundred yards deep. In Sid's life there have been only two fatalities from tiny people falling into this chute, despite the numerous signs warning them of the danger of getting too close to the edge.

The nourishment freefalls down the chute and lands at the bottom with a great thud on the floor of a huge closed tank in your stomach. Access to empty and clean the tank is via a small hatch at the front, at floor level.

Kevin, the kitchen (aka stomach) manager, is responsible for managing your stomach, the insiders call the 'kitchen'. This is the place where the nourishment is further processed on tabletops by Kevin's team. There is an assortment of pots, pans and kitchen type implements available to all staff in that department. The processed nourishment is then packaged and distributed to the various organs of your body via the nourishment tubes, small pipelines you call blood vessels.

So, there you have it. Your Alimentary Tract.

*

Let's now jump back to about fifteen minutes before Sid poured the contents of the take-away trays onto a plate for his tea.

Inside, Kevin is holding a staff meeting during a quiet time in their schedule.

It is approximately four forty-five p.m. and although tea time is rapidly approaching, Kevin needs to hold his daily staff meeting to find out if there are any problems with Sid's digestive system. Mick, the masher, and Fred, the food shoveller, are also present, having been called down to the kitchen by Kevin.

Kevin begins, as he usually does, with a homily about his team's zone of responsibility.

"Good afternoon, everyone. Please take a seat. I'd like to start by reminding you all about the importance of the work we do.

"Fred, have you turned the conveyor off?"

"Yep, all done, and Mick's put the masticator into standby in case the great and almighty Sid decides to snack on something before tea."

Mick waved his hand in the air from the back of the gathering to acknowledge the accuracy of Fred's response to Kevin.

"Good. Okay, folks, let me start by reminding you all that without us, Sid would be in a great deal of trouble. He would need to reside in some hospital or home with a plastic tube permanently attached to his arm to provide simulated liquid nourishment to one of his small pipelines. He wouldn't be able to play football, or travel on a train, or drive a car or make love to Sara without having to lug around a bag full of processed nourishment. Now that's not good, is it?"

Everyone murmured to a neighbour and shook their heads in agreement.

"Okay, so we all know that the job we do, albeit hard and sometimes stressful, is just as important to us as it is to Sid. What I mean by that is if Sid gets ill, or even dies, as a result of *our* negligence, then *we* will suffer the same fate. Is that clear?"

Another murmur from the throng, this time with lots of heads nodding in agreement.

"Good. Now, is everything okay in your departments? Do you need anything? Do any of you need a call from the maintenance chaps?"

A chap in chef's dress stood up and asked, "Can I have a fresh supply of knives, please? Mine have been honed almost to the hilt."

"No problem," answered Kevin, "I'll get another set to you straight away. Any more questions?"

A woman in the centre of the crowd held up her hand and spoke after Kevin pointed to her. "I heard a rumour going round that Sid has been down to the take-away to give Sara a break from cooking. Do we know what he bought?"

"No, not yet, but I'm sure Lee in lookout will let us know as soon as he knows."

Kevin panned the room, with eyebrows raised, for another question.

The chap in chef's dress stood up again and asked "Can we put in a request for Brian to suggest to Sid that he needs to drink more water? Quite a lot of the nourishment passed down to us is bulky and requires a lot of work processing it for distribution. With more fluid in his diet I wouldn't need to sharpen my knives as often."

This raised lots of mumblings and head nods.

"Yes, a good point. I'll put it to Brian as soon as we have finished here. Any more?"

Another woman stood up to ask something, but before she could voice any words the Tannoy system blared out a message from Lee in lookout;

"This is an emergency announcement to all departments. INCOMING! All departments prepare for an excessive input of nourishment. All departments should mobilise reserve staff to their stations immediately and stand by for instructions from Brian regarding an imminent overload of nutrition. THIS IS NOT A DRILL. THIS IS AN EMERGENCY! IMMEDIATE ACTION IS REQUIRED BY ALL DEPARTMENTS!"

The silence in the room following the announcement was deafening. The crowd all looked around with open mouths, waiting for something to happen.

Kevin suddenly ordered, "You heard! Get to it… NOW!

The activity inside Sid suddenly became manic. Chairs got knocked over, people bumped into each other in their haste to go somewhere, small groups formed to hurriedly discuss tactics. Tiny reserve people were turfed out of bed. Those already on duty began running around like headless chickens to collect emergency procedures from the shelves of their departments. Many sat at their desks frantically tapping away on their keyboards, some making urgent phone calls. Utter chaos!

Mick and Fred dashed to the elevator to take them back up to their department.

Elsewhere, all the department managers loudly barked orders to anyone not moving fast enough and an atmosphere of controlled bedlam ensued. To cope with the anticipated influx of reserve staff, additional equipment was carried into the departments so as to be prepared for the overload of nourishment that Lee had warned them about.

Everyone inside made haste to prepare things for the anticipated excessive input of nourishment.

Fred dashed out of the elevator and fired the conveyor into life. He then collected several garden forks, shovels and brooms from his store in readiness for the work he and his team were about to be faced with.

Just as Sid stuffed a fork full of duck breast, dunked in ginger sauce, into his mouth Mick dashed to his consol and pressed the appropriate buttons to put the masticator under his control.

The masticator jumped out of standby and started to chew and grind the duck breast.

Sid is enjoying his meal...

Chapter 5
(The manhole is full)

Inside, the first of Sid's excessive nourishment had been mashed, swept up by Fred's team and shovelled onto the conveyor belt where it was carried to the back of his mouth and dropped down the chute.

Down, down, down the nourishment dropped until SPLAT, it landed on the floor of the collection tank. By the time this had arrived another load was on its way down the chute.

Downstairs the kitchen team sweated profusely as they hurriedly processed the huge pile of nourishment that had started to overflow the collection tank and spill into a heap on the floor of the kitchen. And more was on its way...

Upstairs, Mick's masher had to be moved up a gear because Sid didn't pause between mouthfuls of duck breast followed by some chow mein, then some more duck breast, this time accompanied by a topping of egg fried rice, followed by a couple of aromatic king prawns - Mmmm! Delicious - then a helping of pan-fried scallops with a stick of pork satay bringing up the rear.

"KEVIN!" shouted one of the chefs. "Get a message to Brian to tell Sid to slow down, will you. We can't keep up."

Upstairs and downstairs the teams heaved and shovelled and chopped and processed and packed and swept up and then heaved some more and shovelled some more and processed some more and packed some more and then swept up again. The atmosphere at both levels was manic.

Kevin tapped out a message to Brian on his keyboard:

URGENT MEMO

From: Kevin in kitchen
To: Brian in brain
This message was sent with High importance

Re: Overworked Department

Sid is ploughing through his meal too fast for the team to keep up. If he doesn't slow down soon he'll cause a lot of damage down here.
DO SOMETHING TO STOP SID EATING!
The manhole is full. We can't cope with any more nourishment down here until this backlog has been cleared.

Kevin.

I don't think I mentioned Sid's Intestines, did I?

I'm not going to go into the anatomy of your intestines because I'm in the middle of a sandwich. Suffice to say that the Duodenum - the kitchen staff call this the manhole - is the start of the waste disposal chute, the pipeline that delivers your waste down to its exit doorway in your bottom.

I always thought that Duo meant two, or a pair, or a couple. Duo-denum. A pair of denums. Strange that, 'cos there's only one of them, so why give it such a misleading name? Who knows? Anyway, I digress.

A large manhole cover (the Pyloric Sphincter to you educated idiots) seals the manhole at the top of the waste disposal chute between meals. This is so the kitchen staff can have some R&R between meals without having to whiff the waste all the time. The manhole cover is lifted at mealtimes to enable them to dispose of their rubbish.

42

We throw potato peelings, the outer leaves of sprouts, carrot tops, leftovers etc. into our recycling bins, don't we? We should if we don't. The staff in the kitchen in your stomach throws away all the stuff left over after the nourishment has been processed and packed ready for distribution. There's not much nourishment left in the waste by the time the kitchen staff have finished processing - just a soft mushy substance we call shit. It all goes into the manhole and the manhole cover is returned to its resting place after every meal to stop people falling into the manhole and landing in the shit. That's why that well known phrase was coined, you know. Only one tiny person has 'landed in the shit' since Kevin took over because he wrote the procedure for sealing the manhole after every meal, and he makes sure everyone complies.

Okay, back to Kevin's memo.

The kitchen staff have worked at such a speed that the manhole is now full. It follows that if the manhole is full, so is the waste disposal chute that it is connected to.

Brian had another brainwave. That's what he's there for. He worked long and hard for this promotion and his performance certainly proves that he was a good choice.

"Merv," he commanded, "send a spark to Sid's ideas chip to let him know that the waste chute is full and it's time to open the trapdoor."

*

Outside, Sid scoured his plate clean with the remnants of a bread bun, then sat back, belched softly and said to Sara, "I'll just nip to the toilet for a few minutes."

When Sid had disappeared upstairs Sara started to clear the table and load the dish washer. She hid Sid's two cream-filled eclairs and sherry trifle in the fridge.

'He can have those some other time,' she thought.

Sid sat on the toilet. He wasn't feeling too chipper. He had a bit of a sweat on, and his chest felt as if there was a wide elastic band squeezing it. Each time he took a breath the elastic tightened some more. He sat there for, maybe, twenty minutes before Sara noticed his absence.

She and Suzy were watching TV and had forgotten about Sid.

Sara turned to face Suzy. "Hasn't your dad come downstairs, yet?"

"Not seen him," returned a disinterested Suzy.

Sara watched another few minutes of TV before becoming concerned about Sid.

"I'll go and find out what he's doing." She said, and stood to leave the room.

As she reached the doorway Sid appeared from the stairs.

"You okay?" she asked.

"Yeah? Why?"

"You've been gone a long time and I wondered where you were, that's all."

"Oh, right. I was just a bit constipated. It took me a while to get rid of it."

"Serves you right, the size of that meal... And the way you stuffed it down your throat."

"What? I was hungry."

Sara gave Sid one of her disapproving smiles and sat back down to finish the TV programme that had been interrupted. Sid sat next to Suzy on the settee and she linked arms with him and rested her head on his shoulder.

"Do you want your pudding? I've put it in the fridge" enquired Sara.

"Nah. I'll have it tomorrow. I don't feel like it right now."

Sid couldn't help thinking what a beautiful, loving family he had, but he couldn't quite shake the elastic band feeling around his chest. Perhaps a good night's sleep will get rid of it...

Chapter 6
(Rumble, rumble, clunk!)

Mick, the masher, opened his eyes, peered at his alarm clock and groaned.

Today is the day his electronic diary reminded him to carry out a full and detailed inspection of the masticating machinery.

Bad timing... Sid had had a massive tea yesterday, making his tiny community work ultra hard to mash, process and distribute the vast volume of nourishment that he had forced into the hole in the front of his head. It is Sunday, and everyone was having a long lie-in this morning to rest up from Sid's massive meal, but Mick's electronic diary had been set to wake him earlier than usual so that he could finish his inspection before breakfast got under way.

Mick shook Fred, the food shoveller, to wake him. Mick and Fred usually inspect and maintained their machinery at the same time and Mick is always the one to act as Fred's alarm clock.

"What? What do you want?" grumbled Fred.

"Time to get up," replied Mick. "Today is inspection day."

"Forget it. I'm having a lie-in. Go back to bed, Mick."

"No, can't do that. I'm dressed, already. Anyway, Sid's irresponsible meal last night put both our machines under a lot of stress. I heard a knocking just before I turned my machine off and I want to find out what that was."

"So? Do it without me. You don't need me to help you, do you?" Fred turned over and closed his eyes.

Mick shrugged his shoulders and went to put the kettle on for a cup of tea. While he waited for the kettle to boil he powered up his machinery and returned to his tea making while the masticator warmed up. Sid licked his lips and chewed on something invisible while he slept. He was clearly dreaming about last night's meal...

Mug of tea in his hand, Mick returned to his console. For a while the sound coming from the machinery didn't sound out of the ordinary. Then Mick detected a sort of hiccup in the rumble of the machinery.

Rumble, rumble, clunk! Rumble, rumble, clunk! Yep, definitely a problem with the machinery, somewhere. It sounded like it was coming from the upper deck.

At this point, it's worth mentioning that the masticating machinery is a huge hydraulic press, controlled by a program downloaded onto Mick's PC from the servers upstairs in Brian's department. There are thirty-two individually shaped plates on this machine, sixteen on the top deck and sixteen on the bottom deck, all used to cut, shred, tear and crush the nourishment that Sid shoves through the hole at the front of his head. The masticator engine is tiny... But it's powerful enough to move Sid's Lower Mandible up and down and side to side to crush and mash the nourishment. The resultant mush is passed on to Fred, the food shoveller, who shovels it onto his conveyor belt and sends it to the back of Sid's throat to drop down the kitchen chute.

Get the picture? Okay, back to Mick's clunk!

Mick waited 'til the clunk was about to sound then he paused the masticator. The rumbling of the mechanism slowed to a halt. Mick then climbed up a ladder to the top platform to take a closer look at the machinery in that area.

At first, he couldn't see anything wrong. Then he noticed where the clunk was coming from. Towards the back of Sid's mouth a plate on the masticator was buckled and bent. Mick pressed the play button on his remote control and the machinery started up once more. Keeping an eye on the suspect plate he watched Sid's Lower Mandible raise up to his Upper Mandible as if mashing some nourishment. Rumble, rumble, clunk! Rumble, rumble, clunk! Definitely that faulty plate. It will need to be removed as soon as possible.

Mick slid down his ladder, submarine style, and searched his parts store for another plate. He couldn't find one. This meant only one thing… That section of the masticator will need to be put out of action, probably permanently because Mick will be unable to get another plate shipped into Sid's mouth.

Mick returned to his PC and typed out an email to Brian:

From: Mick, the masher
 To: Brian, brain manager
This message was sent with High importance.

Sid has damaged a crush plate on the
masticator. Probably happened last night,
during his tea. I need to put the masticator
off-line while that part of it is permanently
disconnected. Is there any chance of putting
Sid out of action for a while?

Mick.

Later that morning, after all the tiny people had eventually decided to get out of bed, Brian looked at his emails.

Reading the one from Mick he thought *'Mmmm. I know exactly what Sid needs.'*

Brian knows what Sid needs because that's what he's there for. Like I said, he worked long and hard for this promotion and... Anyway, turning back to his keyboard Brian typed a note to Merv, the message wire manager, sat about three desks back from the front row of the desks facing him:

Action Note

From: Brian/Brain manager
To: Merv/Message wire manager

DAMAGE TO THE MASTICATOR

Sid has damaged a masticator crush plate. Please get him to make an appointment with his dentist to put him out of action while Mick fixes the masticator.

Brian.

The email was sent and Merv immediately telephoned Mick to find out the precise location of the damaged crush plate.

"Morning, Mick. Merv here. I've just received an action note to put Sid out of action while you fix a faulty plate on the masticator. Which plate is it?"

"Morning, Merv. It's the first Molar - B6, left."

"Got it. I'll get Sid to visit the dentist. That'll put him out of action for a while."

"Great! Many thanks."

The call was terminated and Merv wrote out a sub-routine for Sid's nerve, number B6 left, to make it uncomfortable for Sid...

Chapter 7
(Half a tooth)

Outside, after such a big meal Sid may have just sidestepped a heart attack. After a peaceful night's sleep he woke up and focussed on his surroundings. He felt great. No elastic band, no indigestion, no heartburn.

Sara, looking as gorgeous as ever, still slept so Sid carefully eased himself out of bed, so as not to disturb her, and had a good scratch everywhere unmentionable whilst on his way to the bathroom for his morning ablutions.

Shower over with, he stood in front of the mirror admiring his physique.

Sid is one of those guys that no matter what, or how much, they eat they never put on any weight, and at the age of thirty-five he was still incredibly good looking - according to him. Loading his toothbrush with toothpaste, he popped the brush into his mouth and started to brush vigorously.

Then it hit him. The pain. The toothache. A tell-tale sign that there was a problem with one of his teeth. Merv's sub-routine to that nerve really kicked in hard.

Sid didn't finish brushing his teeth - the pain was too much. Sucking in a mouth of cold water straight from the tap he winced as the pain from his tooth multiplied to the power of twenty. After spitting out the water he searched for the offending tooth with his tongue. A gentle touch with the tongue confirmed which tooth was giving him some grief and he opened his mouth wide to see if he could see the offender.

There it was... Half of it, anyway! Towards the back of his top row of teeth.

Sid spoke to himself. "I thought that crispy pancake was a bit too crunchy. I bet that happened when I chewed on it." He then silently thought to himself, *'I wonder where the other half of that tooth went,'* knowing full well that he had undoubtedly swallowed it.

His gum continued to throb while he got dressed and went downstairs. While he was showering, Sara had woken up, put on a dressing gown and gone downstairs to prepare breakfast.

"Morning," she cheerfully smiled.

Sid just grunted something along the lines of, "Yeah."

"Oh dear. Had a bad night, have we? Must have been that huge mountain of food you ate." She derided.

"No, it isn't that." replied Sid. "I've split a tooth in half and it's giving me a lot of grief."

"Do you want me to phone the dentist for you?"

"That won't do any good." Sid growled. "I won't get an appointment this side of Christmas. I'll have to find an emergency dentist to see if they can do anything today."

Sara picked up her phone and dialled the NHS 111 helpline. After being given the telephone number for an emergency dentist's surgery she then made an appointment for Sid to be there in about half an hour. In the car, Sid nursed his now swollen and throbbing jaw, willing the traffic lights to stay green as the car approached them.

Good fortune was on Sid's side.

The dentist's surgery was empty. Maybe they were having an admin day, or something, but Sid wasn't complaining. He could see his tooth being repaired much quicker than he anticipated.

Someone called his name. "Mr. Smethers?"

Sid looked up to see a dental nurse smiling at him from a corridor doorway. He stood up and followed the nurse into the long, dark, intimidating twenty-mile long corridor, doors on either side beckoning Sid as if he was a tasty meal. The nurse opened one of the doors and invited Sid to sit in the chair that was leering at him from the centre of the room.

You'll have gathered that Sid doesn't like going to the dentist. He hates the smell, and the reclining chair, and the sudden appearance of a syringe with a ten foot long needle, and the whining noise that the drill makes. Even worse was the pain of the needle being forced into his gum and the heat of the anaesthetic as it shoots out of the needle into his soft tissue.

"You'll just feel a small prick," or, "This won't hurt," or, "This won't take long," the dentist always says. LIAR! It's a massive jab and it does hurt and it takes ages. Dentists clearly have never had to go through this. They always have nice, straight, white film star teeth that never, ever, require any work on them.

"Good morning Mr. Smethers. Tell me what the problem is." The dentist put on his best "See how perfect my teeth are" pearly white smile.

"I've got a rampant toothache," replied Sid.

"Ah, is that why you're here?"

Sid looked all around and behind his chair. This *is* a dentist's surgery, isn't it?

"It's at the back of my mouth. I think I've broken one of my back teeth."

"Okay. Open wide and let's have a look."

What do dentists mean, 'Let's have a look?' - Let *us* have a look. The dentist is the only one to 'have a look'. There is no *'us'* involved. The nurse certainly never looks

55

when the dentist asks that. She's too busy filling out the invoice for this visit.

Anyway, Sid opened his mouth and the dentist pushed a small circular mirror and a probe-like thing into his mouth.

"Ah, yes. I can see what the problem is. I'm afraid the rest of that tooth will have to come out," said the dentist.

Sid couldn't answer because the dentist was still holding the mirror and probe in his mouth. He just nodded once.

The dentist turned his back on Sid and fiddled with something on a small table. Sid didn't see this 'cos the reclining chair was facing away from the dentist. The nurse busied herself with a rubber bib and some tissues and a cup of cold water and some tinted goggles while Sid pictured the torture he was about to be put to.

The dentist turned round and advised, "I'll be as quick as I can, but just raise your hand if you want me to stop."

The needle appeared in front of Sid's face and he immediately raised his hand.

The needle disappeared from sight.

"I haven't started, yet, Mr. Smethers."

"Oh, yes… No, I was just getting my elbow comfortable," lied Sid.

"Okay. Are you ready now?"

"Yes."

The needle reappeared and Sid closed his eyes in anticipation of the explosion that was about to take place inside his mouth.

"Just relax, and open wide."

Without opening his eyes, Sid visualised the needle being lined up and steered towards the bit of gum supporting what was left of his offending tooth. Then the needle pierced his gum and the plunger started its trajectory down to the bottom of the syringe casing.

From Sid's position the pain was excruciating. From the dentist's position the pain couldn't have been as bad, 'cos all he said was "There. That wasn't so bad, was it?"

LIAR!

Now, one of the reasons that Sid hates going to the dentist is that the anaesthetic rarely works for him until about ten minutes after the injection. Two minutes after this particular injection the dentist asked "How's that, now?" and without waiting for a reply he pulled Sid's lower jaw down and started to extract the tooth.

*

Inside, the anaesthetic effectively knocked out all power to the masticator and plunged the area into darkness. This was Mick the masher's cue to don his head torch and dismantle the offending machinery parts.

He worked quickly and efficiently. He's carried out similar procedures a couple of times before, when one of the masticator's timber parts had rotted through and needed filling, so he is good at it. In no time at all the damaged area of masticator was dismantled and the space left was bypassed with something Mick had constructed to get the machinery up and running again.

*

Outside, the dentist straightened himself upright and ordered Sid to rinse.

"Finished," he said. "That wasn't so bad, after all, was it?"

Liar!

"You'll be able to take the cotton pad out of your mouth when your gum has stopped bleeding. It won't be too long, but keep an eye on it for the time being. Don't chew on that side of your mouth until the wound has completely healed."

Sid departed from the dentist - minus a tooth…

Chapter 8
(Birds are really, really picky)

Sid and Sara are both thirty-seven years old.

They got married seventeen years ago. For the benefit of anyone that is rubbish at maths this means that they got married when they were twenty years old.

At twenty years old, Sid was as randy as most males of that age and when he first got to know Sara he couldn't wait to get inside her pants. She was, after all, the best looking girl around... Still is, if it comes to that. The point is, with a girlfriend like Sara, Sid had lots of shower exercise to practice the transfer of his tadpoles (aka Sperm) all the way up from his ball bag to Sara's arrival lounge.

Now, I could go into a long and detailed explanation of the anatomy and mechanics of the male reproductive system, but I'm not going to. It's far too complicated. There are words and phrases like 'Spermatozoa' and 'Seminiferous Tubules' and 'Rete Testes' and 'Corpus Spongiosum' and 'Navicular Fossa' and a whole truck load of other anatomical and physical features that I'm sure you're not interested in.

Something else... If you have children of your own you will be old enough to know how babies are made - the physical stuff I mean, so I'm not going to go down that path either. If you don't know, by now, you must be incredibly sheltered from the facts of life or you are too young to know. In either case don't ask any of your parents or your teacher. They will give you a lot of spiel about the birds and the bees and they might even enter the world of anatomy and physiology so you still won't know, and you won't have a clue what they're talking about, either. It's much better to ask your older brother. He'll be far more descriptive than anybody else. If you don't have an older brother - tough! You'll have to find out for yourself, but you'll definitely have some fun finding out...

Anyway, I digress.

Think of me as your older brother. The one you have just asked, "How are babies made?" I'm going to keep things nice and simple by starting with the aquarium.

Yes, there is an aquarium inside Sid's body and this is managed by Axel, the aquarium manager. The aquarium sits over the end of every bloke's Vas Deferens and the beginning of his final exit chute.

Now, Axel has a relatively easy job to do. All day he can sit back, relax, and keep an eye on the millions of tadpoles swimming around inside the aquarium, just waiting for him to open the floodgates to allow the tadpoles to begin their difficult journey to a waiting egg that a woman has produced. Axel has named and labelled every one of those tadpoles and the database of names has been sent to Brian in readiness for the time that Sid needs to name his offspring. At the appropriate time, Brian will instruct his message manager to send a suggestion to one of Sid's ideas chips to give Sid a clue as to what name to suggest to Sara, but Brian can't do that until he knows what sex the baby is.

I make no exaggeration by referring to the tadpole's journey as 'difficult'.

There's a saying that goes something like *'The strong shall live and the weak shall die.'* I heard this a lot when I was in the army. I reckon that this dictum has been conceived from the animal kingdom.

TV documentaries tell us that it is always the strongest of the species that survive.

Take birds, for instance. From what I've seen on the TV female birds are really, really picky. One could even go as far as to say that they are demandingly fussy in their choice of a mate. They cavort around and entice any male birds of the same species in the vicinity to "...come and get me," by showing off their best bits and being picky about who they want to have sex with. Why do they do that? Because they want the strongest, most handsomest male bird available to impregnate them with the strongest, most handsomest tadpole.

The weeds in the flock of birds are discarded just like the weeds in your garden. If a weed really wants a mate, he has to work hard at his profile to improve his strength and good looks so as to attract a gorgeous female when the females start to cavort around and strut their best bits.

Most animals are exactly the same. Weeding out the weak ones so that the strongest shall perpetuate the line of that particular species. It's all down to evolution.

Okay, humans are no different. It's true. Compare my portrayal of birds to a usual Saturday night out on the town. Women, also, cavort around and entice any males in the vicinity to "...come and get me," by showing off their best bits and being picky about who they want to have sex with. Presumably, that's why women have been given the holistic slang name of 'birds'. Who knows?

This scenario is played out time and time again. I bet you've never heard anyone say 'Look at that thin, weedy looking bloke with an ugly mush... Don't you just want him to drag you upstairs and throw you on the bed?'

On the other hand, if a woman refers to some bloke she has never met before as a 'hunk', you can bet your trousers that he will share some strong, handsome tadpoles with her, long into the night…

I've said this before, but quite what the gorgeous Sara saw in average Sid is impossible to guess, but they got together, anyway.

Chapter 9
(The beginning of a difficult journey)

So, back to Sid's tadpoles' difficult journey.

On the night of Sid and Sara's wedding they went up to their hotel bedroom and left the wedding revellers to drink some more and chat some more and eventually go home.

Up to the day that Sid and Sara married, Lee, the listening manager (not to be confused with Lee, the lookout manager), had recorded every one of Sid and Sara's conversations about making a baby. Tonight, the actual date for this event, had been previously marked with a red star to highlight its importance. Those recordings have all been sent to Brian, the brain manager, for him to prepare for this particular time. Brian, in turn, has distributed a memo to the following relevant staff:

- Blaire, the ball bag (aka testes) manager. In charge of tadpole manufacture.

- Edgar, the Epididymis manager, Responsible for measuring and categorising the tadpoles.

- Axel, the aquarium manager. In charge of tadpole storage, health and welfare.

- Eddie, the exit chutes manager (aka Vas deferens and Urethra).

- Merv, the message wires manager.

INTERNAL MEMO

From: Brian/Brain manager
To: All staff in Sid's reproduction department.
c.c.: Kevin/kitchen & Merv/message wires
This message was sent with High importance.

Re Advanced Notification

Will all staff please ensure that Sid's reproductive system is running smoothly. We don't want any hiccups when the time comes for Sid and Sara to make a baby.

Blaire - ensure that Axel has a plentiful supply of strong, healthy and handsome tadpoles.

Edgar - your filing system must be up-to-date and capable of accepting millions of tadpole data.

Axel - Please make sure that when the time comes your release hatch must open effortlessly so as to release all tadpoles in one go.

Eddie - check, and doublecheck that the exit chutes are spotlessly clean. We do not want any contaminants affecting the quality or free passage of the tadpoles.

Merv - on my mark send a 'Go' to Eddie to inflate Sid's final exit chute to enable all tadpoles to exit and meet up with Sara's egg.

Eddie, ensure that the inflation engine has an ample supply of fuel. The egg will decide which tadpole to allow entry into its inner chamber.

Get to it, team. Let's help Sid and Sara make a strong, healthy and handsome baby.

Brian.

Inside, the team got to work. Blaire, the ball bag manager, was rushed off his feet manufacturing several batches of tadpoles and the rest of the team cleaned, scrubbed, re-organised and prepared for each batch as it arrived in their department.

Brian cc'd his email to Kevin in the kitchen, with a request for Kevin to increase processing for the nutrients required to produce healthy and handsome tadpoles.

Kevin confirmed, and also informed Eddie, the exit chutes manager, that extra nutrients would be sent to the inflation engine.

Blaire sent batches of tadpoles to Edgar to measure, weigh and categorise. The weak ones were returned to Blaire for more body-building work. From Edgar the tadpoles were stored in the aquarium at the head of the final exit chute for Axel to nurture and train. Eddie had cleaned and polished all the exit chutes and had repeatedly tested the inflation engine, during Sid's morning shower, to ensure that Sid's final exit chute would inflate when it was required.

Outside, Sid and Sara prepared for their night of love making with eager anticipation.

Chapter 10
(Open the gates)

Let's cut to the chase. Wedding ceremony is over, reception is over, the guests have left the hotel to go home and in the privacy of Sid's hotel bedroom Sid and Sara are probing each other's tonsils in a loving embrace.

Clothes get discarded (rapidly!), the bedsheets get peeled back (even more rapidly!), and foreplay is over (extremely rapidly!).

It is time for Sid and Sara to make a baby, something they have discussed for weeks, now, and it has been decided that tonight is the night to do just that. They have practised on each other - quite a lot, although Sara has curtailed activity in that line for about a month because she stopped taking the pill. It goes without saying that they are, right now, both eager to make a baby!

Sid and Sara make passionate love long into the night.

*

Weeks ago, the tadpoles had already started their journey from Sid's ball bag.

Like a horde of football fans that have just departed from the railway station, they were herded, by Blaire, towards Edgar at the head of the Epididymis for categorisation. The fittest and best looking tadpoles were placed into Axel's aquarium, positioned on a platform at the start of Sid's final exit chute, with the release hatch facing a long drop to outside. Axel fed and trained the ones in the aquarium. He put them through their paces to build up their strength for the journey ahead. They were all now 'as fit as a butcher's dog', as the saying goes, each one like a single soldier that has been assembled from a selection of the fittest and most handsome members of the SAS and Parachute Regiment and Royal Marines. A super strong and super handsome tadpole with a tail that could easily whip a bowl of milk into thick cream.

On the wedding night, as soon as Brian gave the word, Eddie, the exit chute manager, fired up the inflation engine. Shortly after the final exit chute had been inflated and put to work by Sid, Brian, via the Tannoy in the room holding the aquarium, shouted out an instruction to Axel.

"OPEN THE GATES. OPEN THE GATES, NOW!"

Axel opened the floodgates and the tadpoles exited the aquarium and landed on the floor of the Epididymis like a box of marbles that had just been tipped over. The tadpoles regrouped into a mass of wriggling bodies. Chatting and laughing and joking in anticipation of a meeting with one of Sara's eggs. Word had got round that this particular egg had been schooled at Sara's Finishing School for Debutant Eggs and that she was a cracker. Best looking egg in the bunch.

The super fit, super handsome tadpoles all dashed to the exit tunnel to start their long and arduous journey to the outside, elbowing each other out of the way so as to be first in the queue.

It was difficult right from the word go. The first thing they had to deal with was the long and bumpy fall down the body of the Epididymis. Not all of them survived. They then had that long, steep climb up to the plateau of the Vas Deferens. Several were unable to make it to this point. Here, the tadpoles were afforded a brief rest before barging past each other to get to the downward trajectory that they had been told about - a shorter slide downwards to the Seminal Vesicle where Eddie was waiting with cartons of water, like a helper on the route of a marathon.

The tadpoles were re-categorised by Eddie and the weakest of them were returned for retraining.

Pandemonium ensued as the passage to the final exit chute (aka Urethra and Ejaculatory duct) suddenly became extremely narrow. There was just enough room for, perhaps, a couple of million tadpoles to squeeze into. This caused a mighty bottleneck and many weary tadpoles were pushed and fell and got crushed in the mad dash to get to the final exit chute. At the top of the final exit chute the chatting and laughing and joking was now substituted with angry shouts of "Get out of the way!" and fights broke out as the tadpoles struggled and climbed over dead bodies to reach the final exit chute. Dozens more tadpoles were eliminated from the race.

The remaining tadpoles dived into the final exit chute and they were suddenly projected out of Sid's body into the waiting arrival lounge in Sara's insides. Many more died in that moment of jetting out of Sid and into Sara.

Eddie, in particular, had the difficult job of keeping Sid's final exit chute inflated for the whole period. He got some help from Sara, but at about three-thirty in the morning his inflation engine ran out of fuel. It was just as well, because Sid and Sara had decided that they had had enough tries at making a baby, and they both rested weary heads on pillows and closed their eyes.

The tadpoles now inside Sara went on the hunt for an egg - any egg - that would permit entry into its inner chamber, but preferably the one that had been to the Finishing School for Debutant Eggs.

The carnage didn't end even though Sid and Sara slept.

Having overcome the final hurdle of being fired from Sid, the remaining million tadpoles barged and elbowed and jostled and shouted at each other to "Make way...!" for them to get to Sara's egg, now lounging in wait for the strongest and most handsome of the tadpoles. More fights broke out to get to the egg and a few more were eliminated. Like I said - just like a usual Saturday night out on the town!

The egg is now surrounded by wriggling, squirming tadpoles, all pleading to be let in to her inner chamber. She takes her time in choosing just the right one. The fittest and most handsomest and, indeed, the most persuasive. When she makes up her mind which tadpole she fancies the most she lets him in.

Yep! Exactly like the usual Saturday night... The strong shall live and the weak shall die.

And that's how Susy was made.

Chapter 11
(Moules Marinière... Mmmm)

It is summer time. Time for Sid, Sara and Suzy to go on holiday, get sand between their toes, soak up some sun, enjoy some zzz's, eat too much cholesterol, drink too much alcohol and generally enjoy themselves.

Suzy is usually too embarrassed by Sid and Sara to spend much time with them. Sid insists on sporting ridiculous t-shirts with ridiculous phrases on them, and Sara cavorts around in nothing but a throng to please Sid. He's not concerned about the packs of suave, wavy haired, face-full-of-white-teeth and all smiling wolves that follow Sara around with their age old spiel about having a drink somewhere quiet. Sid is confident that Sara will not stray from the straight and narrow because she and Sid genuinely adore each other and absolutely refuse to let anything come between them.

At the first available opportunity Suzy heads out on her own to find a suave, wavy haired, face-full-of-white-teeth and all smiling wolf her own age. She also cavorts around in nothing but a throng because she has learned from Mum that that is what attracts suave, wavy haired, face-full-of-white-teeth and all smiling wolves. She usually waits until Sid and Sara are out of sight before removing her thin nylon wrap to expose her assets to the sun.

Anyway, Sid booked a week in a plush hotel in Morocco. Ironically, the hotel is on the beachfront in Tangiers, of all places. You'll find out how ironic in a moment.

The travel agent had booked a mid afternoon flight, departing from Heathrow at one fifty-five p.m., so Sid and his family didn't arrive at the hotel until well after the last call for dinner. In fact, the restaurant was empty.

Booked into their rooms, suitcases emptied and clothes hung up, the family met down in the foyer to discuss dinner.

Sid enquired about available restaurants in the area but, unfortunately, was told that today, being a state holiday in Morocco, it would be extremely unlikely that any restaurant would be open. Disappointed faces all round, but Sid was not one to give up easily. Taking out his wallet he flashed about three hundred Moroccan Dirhams at Sahila, the hotel receptionist.

"How much will it cost to persuade the chef to work a bit later than normal?"

The receptionist's eyes lit up.

"Er, I don't know that, precisely, sir, but I know where I can find him to ask."

"What are you waiting for?"

The receptionist trotted off to find the chef, and Sara approached Sid.

"Do you think he can arrange a meal?" she asked.

"Don't know yet but I bet he will come back with some good news."

Suzy piped up in her usual angry teenager whinge, "When are we going to get something to eat, Dad? I'm starving."

With a look of disapproval, Sara answered, "Just wait a moment Suzy. Your dad's doing his best."

Suzy retreated back into her own world muttering something along the lines of, 'Not good enough...' but nobody heard her because they weren't really taking any notice of what she said.

The receptionist soon re-appeared with Siham, the chef, in tow.

"Good evening, sir. How can I help you?"

"We've just arrived. Is there any way you can crack up a quick meal for us?" waving his hand at Sara and Suzy.

"Unfortunately, sir, the kitchen and restaurant have been closed for the night."

Sid took out his wallet, once more, and tapped the fingers on his other hand with it. "Is it possible to open the kitchen and restaurant... Temporarily? For cleaning, I mean..."

"I can see no reason why not, sir," eyeing the wallet, "but it may be expensive."

Sid took out a wad of notes and tapped them on the wallet. "Would two hundred Dirham cover the cleaning bill?"

"You realise that today is a state holiday, don't you, sir?"

Sid eyeballed the chef for a second or two. "Three hundred?" he proffered.

"Three hundred and seventy-five would cover the additional expense of replacing the tablecloth with a clean one, sir."

Sahila chipped in, "... and I would need a commission for my services. Call it a finder's fee, if you like."

Sid looked disapprovingly at Sahila and said, "I don't like, but you're in. You get a ten percent commission."

"Very well, sir. Would you and your family like to follow me?" Sahila smiled, grabbing the wad of notes out of Sid's hand before Sid had a chance to change his mind.

Much to everyone's relief they were hidden away on a nice corner table, out of view from where somebody else might see them and want a snack.

The chef accompanied the family to the table, then suggested the 'Chef's Speciality'; Moules Marinière in white wine with a side dish of Oysters sautéed in a wine sauce and topped with asparagus. A bottle of chilled white wine would be served up with the main meal. To follow, Crème brûlée.

"I'm afraid it is the only meal that I can quickly prepare for you at such short notice," apologised the chef.

Sid and his family nodded in agreement. They were too hungry and too tired to argue against it.

Meal over with, and after a couple of drinks and a chat, Sid and his family retired to their hotel rooms for some sleep. They didn't get much...

Chapter 12
(…and the bugs multiplied)

Inside, a weary Brian, brain manager, was called from his own bed almost immediately Sid had finished his 'Chef's Special'. In his jim-jams and slippers Brian entered the control room.

"What's the problem?" he asked his 2IC (aka Second-in-Command).

"It's Sid's kitchen," replied the 2IC. "I've just had a call from Kevin to ask you to make an urgent visit down there."

"Oh? Did he say why?"

"No, only that it was imperative you get down there as soon as possible."

Brian turned to the rest of the duty night staff. "Can anyone lend me a coat to save me going back to my room?"

A woman stood and dragged her coat from the back of her chair. It was a fetching pink coat with a fluffy collar and fluffy sleeves and a red bow at the back. Brian stared at the coat as it floated across the room to him.

"Is that it? Hasn't anyone got something more appropriate for me to wear to the kitchen?"

No replies.

With a huge portion of trepidation Brian put the coat on.

"If I see, or hear, anyone laughing you will all be on night duty for the rest of your lives. Every one of you!"

The night staff all looked at the floor to hide their smiling faces, shoulders bobbing up and down as they tried to suppress their chuckles. Brian took the lift down to the kitchen with a face as black as thunder. He didn't like being woken up at the best of times, but to visit another department wearing this coat was the limit. As soon as the lift doors closed the brain department burst into fits of laughter.

The lift doors opened and Brian stepped out. Everything went quiet. Brian scanned the room to find Kevin, but the sight of a pretty pink coat with blue striped jim-jams and brown slippers protruding from its hem was just too much for the kitchen department's night staff to ignore.

"You there! What are you laughing at?" demanded an angry Brian.

"Er, nothing sir," answered the keyboard operator who immediately buried his face into his PC screen after answering.

Brian sighed an angry sigh. He noticed that the lift had dropped him off on a different floor to the kitchen department. This place seemed to be some kind of emergency planning room, with charts on the walls and a large central table showing a map of the Gastrointestinal Tract. Like a war room. People were busily chatting in front of and pointing at terminals. Others were pinning pins onto the wall charts and a core, standing round the central table, were repositioning tiny toy-like markers with long sticks. Lighting was low and there was a sense of urgency in everyone's actions.

Kevin looked back from what he was doing on the central table and hurried up to Brian. Quite how he managed to approach Brian with a straight face is anybody's guess.

"Thanks for coming down Brian. I'm sorry you had to be disturbed."

"Get on with it, Kevin. What's the problem?"

"You need to see this," said Kevin, ushering Brian to a terminal. "Fred, the food shoveller sent down a video of what happened as soon as Sid started his meal last night."

Kevin tapped a key and the video started to play. What Brian saw horrified him.

*

Cut to the video.

Mick, the masher, was watching the masticator masticating. Fred, the food shoveller, was shovelling nourishment onto the conveyor belt.

A mashed up chunk of marinated mussel dropped out of the masticator onto the floor of the Oral Cavity and the masticator was reloaded, by Sid, with an oyster. Before Fred could do anything with the chunk of mussel, it morphed into a sort of piled up dollop of jelly that suddenly collapsed into a mass of billions of writhing, heaving bacteria bugs. That particular mussel was most probably undercooked, and the personal hygiene of the chef is definitely questionable! More ominously, the bacteria bugs started to multiply.

There was no way that Fred was going to let this mass of bacteria bugs mess up his space, all laughing and joking and celebrating as if they were enjoying a huge new year's party. No way.

Thinking to himself, *'Kevin's department can deal with this lot.'* Fred and his night staff quickly shovelled the bugs onto the conveyor. They had to work quickly because the bugs continued to multiply while they shovelled. Eventually every bug had been conveyed to the back of Sid's mouth and dropped down the chute. The rest of the masticated nourishment was now backing up, so

Fred's team worked themselves into a sweat to clear it. Even Mick joined in the shovelling to help out.

By the time the bacteria bugs had landed on the floor of the tank in the kitchen department there were a few billion more of them... And they continued to multiply! The bugs looked around for some nourishment of their own. As soon as the mashed up oyster landed in the tank the bacteria bugs smothered it, happily munching away to satisfy their appetite... And the bugs continued to multiply.

In fact, they multiplied so much and so quickly that the tank was very quickly overflowing with bacteria bugs. As soon as the overflowed bugs landed on the floor of the kitchen department they began to multiply. They spread out, hunting for some nourishment of their own.

It wasn't long before the department was covered with bacteria bugs, mashed nourishment that had been pushed out of the tank by the multiplying bacteria and bug faeces. The stuff was everywhere, covering the floor, processing tables, walls and ceiling... And the bugs continued to multiply. The department staff had to evacuate the room pretty quickly. Kevin was the last to leave after sending an urgent memo to the brain department asking for Brian's assistance.

As soon as any nourishment landed down the throat chute from Fred's conveyor it was pounced on and devoured by hungry bacteria bugs. By the time the department had been evacuated the bugs had prized open the manhole cover and dived into the manhole, devouring any waste that could be found in the waste chute... And the bugs continued to multiply.

Now, at the very bottom of the waste chute there is a trapdoor. The purpose of this trapdoor is to stop waste material (aka shit) from free-falling into one's pants and being squashed all over the back of one's arse and legs when one sits down. Educated people call this the Anal Sphincter. Sid's tiny people call this the trapdoor.

There are pressure sensors on the outside of the trapdoor, and door release is regulated by a computer program in the kitchen department. When the waste chute begins to fill and pressure builds up against the trapdoor, the computer program sends a signal to the trapdoor to open, but not until Sid is sat in position on the toilet seat. So, the computer program has just a few lines of code that can easily be shown by a simple flow chart. A picture is worth a thousand words, as they say:

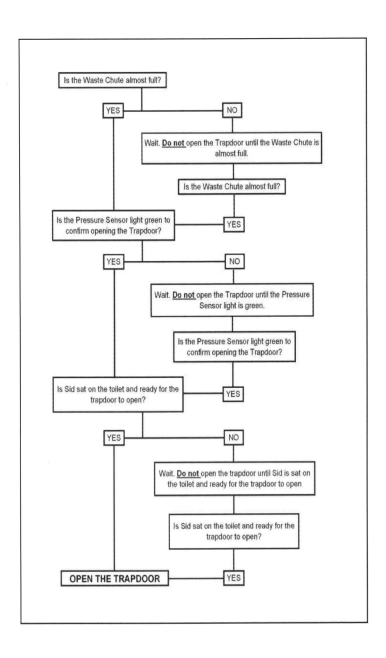

Is the Waste Chute almost full?

YES · NO

Wait. **Do not** open the Trapdoor until the Waste Chute is almost full.

Is the Waste Chute almost full?

Is the Pressure Sensor light green to confirm opening the Trapdoor? · YES

YES · NO

Wait. **Do not** open the Trapdoor until the Pressure Sensor light is green.

Is the Pressure Sensor light green to confirm opening the Trapdoor?

Is Sid sat on the toilet and ready for the trapdoor to open? · YES

YES · NO

Wait. **Do not** open the trapdoor until Sid is sat on the toilet and ready for the trapdoor to open

Is Sid sat on the toilet and ready for the trapdoor to open?

OPEN THE TRAPDOOR · YES

80

*

Cut back to Brian and Kevin.

Brian looked at Kevin. Kevin looked back. Brian suddenly turned and headed towards the lift doors, shouting to Kevin as he ran.

"Send a copy of that video upstairs, Kevin. I'll get back and prepare for what Sid's got heading in his direction. We'd better get the trapdoor open pronto to release all those bugs. They've done enough damage already."

"Copy that," replied Kevin.

The lift returned Brian to the brain department and with any thoughts of embarrassing clothes now at the back of his mind he dashed out of the lift to home in on his 2IC.

"Kevin's just sent a video up to your terminal. Get a copy to all departments and get on to Merv, the Message manager, to crank up his 'ideas' chip to receive some urgent instructions."

"Yes, sir. Already done."

"Good man. Sid's going to need a lot of help from us, soon, so make sure everyone is on the ball."

"Yes, sir. Already done."

Brian telephoned Mick and Fred, down in the oral cavity.

"Mick, are we on a conference line?"

"Yep. Got Kevin's video. Fred and myself have got our place cleaned up and it appears that Sid isn't feeling too well. What do you want us to do?"

"Put on your oilskins and prepare for a tempest..."

81

Chapter 13
(Oooooh!)

Outside, Sid and his family should NOT have eaten those undercooked mussels, but they wouldn't have known that they were undercooked at the time. If they had thought about it, they might have guessed that the meal that had been dished up so rapidly might have had a few 'problematic' characteristics, but they were too tired and too hungry to consider such things.

Neither would they have known that the chef's personal hygiene left a lot to be desired.

Here's the irony that I skipped over earlier.

Unfortunately, food poisoning has descended on the whole family. Gastroenteritis caused by **Staphylococcus Aureus,** also known as Staph... The 'Tangier trots,' had struck. An appropriate name given that they were in a hotel in Tangiers.

Have you ever *thought* you were going to fart, then found out that it was more than a fart - too late? Despite any response in the negative, I bet you have. Everyone has, and it can be really embarrassing, can't it? What's worse is that sometimes it is more liquid than solid. That wet feeling down the back of your legs is so, what shall we say, warm...

Next question. When you *thought* you were going to fart, then found out that it was more than a fart - too late, what did you say to yourself? I bet it was something along the lines of "Ooo, crap!" or "Aww, shit!" At times like this you tell it how it is.

That's how it started for Sid in the early hours of the morning following the meal.

The bacteria bugs in Sid's intestines had partied and munched and devoured most of the waste in the waste chute, leaving just their urinated fluid and bug faeces. After a disturbed couple of hours of grumble-tum, Sid *thought* that the pressure on his trapdoor was just a fart pushing to escape. Unfortunately, not just for Sid but for Sara, also, condition three of Sid's flow chart was not satisfied. To make matters worse, Sid never wears Pyjamas in bed...

Taking a breath, and without waiting for Brian to give the appropriate command, Sid pushed against his trapdoor until it flew open, supposedly to release what he *thought* was a fart. The whole smelly, liquid content of Sid's waste chute shot out of the trapdoor and into the bed, covering the backs of both Sid and Sara! Shower time, and God knows what the hotel staff were going to say about the bedsheets.

After a shower, Sid and Sara did their best to rinse out the bacteria bugs and bug waste from the sheets and they then dumped the sheets in the bath. They opened the balcony doors to let some of the stench out. I bet the whole of Tangiers assumed that there was a problem with the drains, somewhere, because a smelly, lime green translucent cloud blanketed the whole town.

As soon as Sid and his wife settled down, under just the duvet, Sara suddenly jumped out of bed and dashed to the toilet, squeezing the cheeks of her arse together with her hand to prevent her own trapdoor from flying open.

Things were no better for Suzy. With an abdominal pain that would break all records in the pain barrier, Suzy visited her own toilet to point her face at the toilet bowl and vomit the contents of her stomach into it.

Little sleep was had by any of the family. For the remainder of that night they all experienced the effects of Tangier trots - Nausea, abdominal pain, diarrhoea, vomiting.

Inside, down at the bottom of the waste chute, Tim, the trap door maintenance manager, was giving his right arm, the one he used to operate the lever that manually opened and closed the trapdoor, a good work-out.

The perpetual proliferation of the bacteria bugs kept Fred and Mick busy all night, cleaning up after the bacteria and bug waste as it was constantly forced back up the nourishment chute, through the oral cavity and out through the hole at the front of Sid's face. Sara and Suzy's tiny people fared no better.

The following morning Sid's family decided to give breakfast a miss. They all congregated in Sid's room, each one of them suffering with a fever and headache, muscle aches, weakness and fatigue. Suzy and Sara lay on the bed and moaned while Sid occupied the chair. Suzy was so ill that Sara phoned down to reception to ask for an urgent visit by a doctor... Between visits to the toilet, herself. Sid just sat and moaned.

It wasn't long before Saloua, a doctor from the town, arrived - just a few minutes, actually. He wore a face mask.

Puzzled by the doctor's promptness, Sid asked if he was a hotel resident.

"No. I was already on site when the receptionist instructed me to call here."

"Oh? Why's that?"

"Unfortunately, several of the guests have been struck down, like yourselves, with food poisoning. I'll give you all something that will ease the symptoms, but the effects are unlikely to stop for a while. You must remain in your room for about four days until the effects of the food poisoning have completely disappeared because Staphylococcus Aureus is quite contagious. Drink plenty of bottled water and don't eat anything until

85

tomorrow, at the earliest, or at least until you feel like it...
And then just a light snack, just until you are well again.
Stay away from any shellfish."

The diagnosis provided by the doctor didn't sit well with Lee in listening. As soon as she had recorded the doctor's words of wisdom she sent the sound file up to Brian for his consideration.

After listening to the sound file Brian turned to his message wires manager.

"Merv, send a reminder to Sid's ideas chip to contact his solicitor as soon as possible."

Sid's family holiday was now ruined. With a lockdown in their rooms for four out of the seven days booked for the holiday - more than half the holiday period - there was no way Sid was going to roll over and accept that this was any kind of an accident. Merv's ideas reminder prompted Sid into action. Firing up his laptop, Sid sent an urgent message to his solicitor to contact the travel agents with a view to securing a refund from them.

The chef was dismissed from his position at the hotel.

Chapter 14
(What? Speak up)

Having recovered from the Tangier trots, Sid and Sara tried to rescue the holiday by cramming as much into the remaining three days as they could.

Wally, the wax manager, shares an office with Lee in listening (not to be confused with Lee in lookout). Just before breakfast on the fifth morning Wally and Lee were chatting when they both heard Sid and Sara discussing their day's itinerary.

"How're you feeling today?" asked Sid.

"Much, much better. Do you fancy a bit of snorkelling after breakfast?"

"Not ready for breakfast, yet, but snorkelling is a good idea. It's not too far away from the toilet, if we need it."

"True. I'll let Suzy know what we're doing."

Suzy wasn't one hundred percent, yet, so she mooched around, looking for a suave, wavy haired, face-full-of-white-teeth and all smiling idiot that she could flirt with while Sid and Sara went snorkelling off the beach.

After snorkelling for about half an hour Sid ambled out of the water and returned to his towel, draped over the back of his deck chair. Hair dried, back dried, front dried, armpits dried, legs dried and feet dried, Sid wrapped a bit of towel around his index finger to tackle his right ear.

Ramming his towel covered finger into his ear canal he waggled it up and down to try to soak as much excess water into the towel as possible. After screwing his finger around to force the towel further into his ear canal he pulled it out to tackle his left ear. The towel didn't get a chance to visit the left ear. As soon as Sid's finger was withdrawn from his right ear he knew he had a problem... He was suddenly deaf in that ear.

He immediately knew what the problem was and he tilted his head onto his right shoulder in the hopes that the water would drain out of his ear.

No chance.

I don't know why, but when people get water in their ears they do something really daft. They tilt their head towards the shoulder adjacent to that ear and they then *bang* the opposite side of their head! Why do they do that - bang the side of their head? It doesn't do anything except jolt their brain - much to Brian's annoyance. It certainly doesn't clear any water out of the ear.

Anyway, what's happened to make Sid deaf?

Well, the ear canals are lined with tiny hairs that protect the inner ears by trapping and preventing dust, bacteria, and other germs and small objects from entering and damaging the ears. The ear canals also have glands that secrete a waxy oil called Cerumen... Ear wax.

Now, ear wax doesn't taste very nice, so don't lick your little finger if you've just used it to waggle up and down inside your ear to scratch that itch. Ear wax is there to protect the delicate skin of the ear canal from getting irritated when any water or fine particles get into the canal.

Usually, ear wax makes its way to the opening of the ear - to the External Tragus (aka the point of no return to the outside world) - and it will fall out or be removed by washing, so it doesn't normally cause a problem. It can, however, build up and block the ear canal. If the build-up of wax doesn't block the ear, impacting it with something shoved into the ear will.

Wax blockage is one of the most common causes of deafness.

That's exactly what Sid has just done. He's had a long term build-up of ear wax, without knowing it, and waggling his towel covered finger inside his ear canal has impacted the wax to fully block the canal, trapping some water behind it.

To fix this, now, he will need to see the hotel nurse… Again. It will probably cost Sid an arm and a leg to get the nurse to syringe his ear with a jet of water to clear the blockage, but at least he will be able to hear what's being said.

He told Sara that he was going to see if the nurse was available and then made his way back to the hotel.

*

On a daily basis Wally, the wax manager, exits the office through the isolation door in the wall dividing Sid's Eustachian Tube from his ear canal to clean the tiny hairs and sweep up the dust particles that have been captured by the hairs.

He has noticed, for some time now, that the wax secretion gland in Sid's right ear has been producing more wax than he is comfortable with, but dismantling the gland to service it is a tedious job, and Wally prefers to adopt a reactive management approach to this kind of maintenance.

Let me remind you of that age old adage, *'A stitch in time saves nine',* meaning that it is better to put right something that is wrong *before* it gets worse. Wally could have stripped down the gland before now, but it's a tedious job, isn't it, and Wally thought he could get away with ignoring the wax build-up until after the holiday.

Wrong call!

Sid's conversation to Sara about going to see the hotel nurse rang bells in Wally's head.

"I think the problem with Sid's right ear might be a wax blockage," he volunteered to Lee.

"What makes you think that?"

"Well, I really should have stripped down the wax secretion gland in that ear to give it a good clean, but I thought I would leave it 'til Sid returned from his holiday."

"Oh, great! Brian's not going to be pleased with you, Wally."

"He never is…"

It goes without saying that Wally's laissez-faire attitude has been noted in the past by Brian, and Wally is not, therefore, high up on Brian's list of potential candidates for promotion.

Lee asked Wally, "Do you know what's needed to clear out the blockage, Wally?"

"If Sid is on his way to see the nurse, it's likely that she will syringe his ear out with warm water. That usually does the trick, but I should go and see how serious it is."

"No, don't do that. I'll email Brian to let him know what's happened."

INTERNAL MEMO

From: Lee in listening
To: Brian
c.c.: All relevant staff
This message was sent with High importance.

Re: Sid's right ear.

I thought I would let you all know that the microphone in Sid's right ear is not picking up any sound from the outside.

Wally suggests that the ear canal is blocked with ear wax and that it may need syringing out. We've just heard Sid tell Sara that he is on his way to see the hotel nurse.

Brian, is there anything in standing orders on this issue, and can you please spare me a moment to discuss it?

> *Regards,*
> *Lee.*

Lee and Brian have got something private going on between themselves and the email is really a hidden message for them to meet up, *again*, somewhere private and unseen.

Brian sent out an email of his own:

INTERNAL MEMO

From: Brian/brain manager
To: All relevant staff
This message was sent with High importance.

Re: Advance notification - Possible ear syringe.

It is more than likely that Sid will have his right ear syringed to clear a blockage in that ear. The time of this procedure is, at present, unknown.

Will all staff make a note of Lee's recent message and take appropriate steps to protect Sid from any bacteria that may be lurking in the ear canal.

Daphne - Please report on how Sid's immune system is fairing with the blockage.

Wally - please provide a report on the condition of Sid's wax gland prior to his holiday.

Lee - Ensure that the microphone is bolted down securely and covered, that the barrier door is closed, sealed and locked, and then meet me in Sid's Cochlea Labyrinth to discuss matters further.

Brian.

Lee's hidden message seems to have worked, but nobody is fooled...

Chapter 15
(Help! Let me in!)

Here's the thing... If you don't communicate, you don't know.

Inside, Wally felt a bit guilty about not properly cleaning Sid's right ear wax gland. Despite Lee's instruction, he decided to go out and see what he could do about clearing the blockage. After all, it was partially his fault that the blockage occurred.

Without saying a word to Lee, while she sat at her terminal composing her message to Brian, he went out to Sid's ear canal, quietly closed the door isolating the canal from Sid's Eustachian Tube and disappeared into the blackness of the canal. The wax gland and blockage was somewhere in the region of fifty yards (inside world distance) in the direction of the External Tragus (aka the point of no return to the outside world).

He had not read the message from Brian.

With a torch strapped to his head and a really, really tiny garden spade he approached the wall of wax in front of him, waded through ankle deep water and began to tackle the blockage.

With a smile on her face, Lee finished reading Brian's message and made her way through the canal isolation door and out to the microphone. After checking the mic stand for sturdiness and covering it with a purpose made waterproof bag, she turned round and returned through the canal door, not knowing that Wally was working fifty yards away in the darkness.

Wally didn't hear the door key being turned in its lock, or the bolts being bolted or the door bar being lowered into place. He was too busy trying to clear the blockage.

Lee looked round the empty office.

"Wally? Are you there, Wally?"

"She peered around the office and called out, "Wally? Where are you?"

No reply.

'I bet he's bunked off to see that floozy from the defence force department again. What's her name? Ida. That's her. Ida from the defence force department. Phuh! Some people...' thought Lee, conveniently forgetting about her and Brian. Talking of which, she suddenly remembered that she was due to meet Brian in the Cochlea Labyrinth to '... discuss matters.'

Satisfied that the canal isolation door was secured and sealed, she made her way out of the office and she, also, disappeared into the darkness of the inner ear corridors.

Wally made absolutely no headway into the wall of ear wax that had been compacted from the other side of the ear canal.

After about an hour (inside world time) he sat down with his back to the canal wall to rest for a while. Sitting there, thinking of what pleasures he would enjoy later this evening with Ida, from the immune department, he heard a distant rumbling and felt the floor vibrate slightly. It wasn't a constant rumble. The rumbling was followed by silence.

He turned his head to look at the wall of wax. There it was, again. That rumble, followed by silence.

Wally stood and gently put his ear to the wax wall. Nothing.

Then the rumbling started again. This time he felt the wall vibrate slightly… And he felt a drop of water land on his head. Then silence. He looked up but couldn't see where the water was coming from.

He backed up a few steps and surveyed the wax wall from a distance of about four or five yards (inside world distance) with his arms folded.

"There! There it is! That's where the water is dripping from," he declared out loud, noticing a small hole about two thirds the distance up the wall. Then the rumbling started again, and a few drops of water spat out of the hole.

'What the…?' he thought as the rumbling changed to silence. Then the penny dropped.

"Oh, shit!" he shouted out loud. "Sid's having his ear syringed right now!"

Picking up the spade he turned and started his sprint back to the isolation door.

Another rumbling, this time much louder. The silence that followed was deafening.

Wally sprinted down the ear canal as fast as his legs could go. Then he heard the crash of the wax wall being demolished by the water jet being forced out of the syringe. He urged his legs to run faster - still some distance to go.

The rumbling thundered loud, this time, and he looked backwards to see a floor to ceiling wall of water charging towards him. Then it suddenly collapsed and the water drained back towards the External Tragus. Silence.

Wally reached the isolation door and tried the handle. Locked!

A red light came on and Wally looked at it in horror as he realised that the light was a warning that the door is locked and sealed. With as much force as he could muster he hammered on the door, shouting "LEE! LEE! HELP! OPEN THE DOOR, LET ME IN!"

No response.

He repeated his hammering and his plea for help.

Still no answer.

Another rumbling.

Wally looked round in a panic to see if there was anything to shelter from the jet of water heading in his direction. Nothing. He hammered the door with the spade to attract attention. Nothing.

He saw another wall of water crashing down the canal towards him. He knew that if the door didn't open soon he would be swept down the ear canal to the outside world with absolutely no chance of being able to return back into Sid's ear. He visualised himself being tipped out of an outside world kidney dish into a massive sink and down a huge plughole, to be carried out to who knows where... The thought terrified him and his eyes darted everywhere, desperately searching for somewhere to hide.

The wall of water was now just a few yards away and menacingly approaching at speed. Any second now the water will crash over his head and drag him to the outside world!

He stood with his back against the door, his defiant stance almost mocking the wall of water about to sweep him away to the unknown.

Lee returned to her office after 'chatting' with Brian about Sid's ear. She had been absent for about an hour and a half (inside world time) and on returning to her desk she noticed that Wally had still not returned.

Slightly puzzled, she picked up the phone and dialled the immune department.

"Defence force department," answered Daphne, the defence force manager.

"Hi, Daphne. It's Lee from listening here. Can I have a quick word with Ida?"

"Yeh, sure. Anything wrong?" asked Daphne.

"No, not at all. I'm just making sure Ida is still coming to my place later, to play some cards."

"Oh, Okay. IDA? PHONE!" shouted out Daphne, and Lee heard the phone being laid on the desk...

"Ida speaking."

"Hi, Ida. Is Wally down there with you?"

"No... Not seen him since yesterday. Why?"

"Oh, it's probably nothing. He bunked off this afternoon and I need to see him about something."

"Okay. Tell him he owes me for last night and that I intend to collect."

"Yeh, will do," answered Lee, not really wanting to know what Wally 'owed' her, or why. "Are you still on for tonight?" she asked.

"Of course," answered Ida.

Lee put the phone back in its cradle.

'Maybe he decided to get some sleep if he had a long night, last night.' thought Lee, and then decided to check on the situation regarding Sid's ear syringe. She booted up her PC and called up the activities menu. Scrolling down to this afternoon's activities she homed in on the maintenance folder.

Yep. The ear has been syringed and the wax situation is now stable. The wax gland is now clean and it is safe to remove the microphone covers.

'*Great!*' thought Lee. '*Wally must have been busy this afternoon.*'

She emailed Brian:

INTERNAL MEMO

From: Lee in listening
To: Brian

Re: Sid's ear

Have you been told if Sid's right ear has been syringed, yet? I'm ready to remove the microphone covers.
Thanks for the chat earlier. I feel much better, now.

Lee.

Brian replied immediately:

INTERNAL MEMO

From: Brian/Brain manager
To: Lee in listening

Re: Sid's ear

Yep. Ear syringed while we were chatting It's safe to go out and remove the covers.
Glad you were pleased with the chat.

Brian.

With a smile, Lee logged off and went to unlock the isolation door. As soon as she approached it she noticed the red light above the door blinking at her.

'Uuh? Has somebody been trying to get in?'

The terrible answer hit her like a runaway bus.

"Wally!" she said out loud with concern in her voice.

As quickly as she could to turn the key, unbolt the bolts and remove the door bar she realised that if Wally had been out there when the ear was being syringed it was unlikely that he would still be there now.

Yanking the door open she dashed out shouting his name.

"WALLY! WALLY!"

No reply.

Her heart sank. How was she going to let the others know what happened? That she had locked Wally out of the inner ear and he had been washed away by the onslaught of water.

She was devastated. Heartbroken. Sobbing, she made her way to the microphone to remove the cover.

'They will never forgive me,' she thought. *'What can I say to them? To Brian - he will have to relocate me. He won't want to see me again.'*

With sadness and tears she approached the microphones... And found Wally wrapped around a microphone stand. The stand was bent towards the ear canal, pointing outwards, towards the point of no return.

Kneeling over Wally she lifted his arm from the twisted metal of the mic stand.

"I'm sorry, Wally," she wept, lifting and cradling his lifeless head in her arms. "I should have checked more thoroughly. I didn't know you were out here. I'm so sorry," tears falling onto his hair.

"And so you should be…" answered Wally.

Lee froze. Her face lowered to look into Wally's now open eyes.

"What?… What?… You're alive?"

"Never felt better."

"WHAT?"

"Never felt better - or cleaner. You've got lovely eyes. Do you know that?"

Lee dropped Wally's head on the floor with a bump as she stood up.

"You let me think you were dead, you rotten sod!"

"I nearly was, for a moment. It wasn't until you lifted my head that I was able to take a proper breath." He sat up and propped his back against the twisted mic stand. "It's a good job these things are bolted to the floor. Otherwise I would have been well on my way to the ocean by now."

"Bastard!" was all that Lee could say as she turned and headed towards the isolation door. "I've a good mind to lock this door again. Then see how cocky you are."

Wally smiled. Lee was mad with him right now, but she will forgive him when she's calmed down.

Chapter 16
(The egg hotel)

Do you recall me suggesting 'that's how Susy was made' after telling you about Sid's tadpoles?

Well, that statement wasn't exactly true. It was only half the story. Let's look at the other half.

Sara also has an army of really, really tiny people working in departments inside her that are similar to those of Sid's. But we all know that men and women are different, don't we? If you need to ask how men and women are different you're not old enough to read this book...

So, remember that evolutionary saying, *'The strong shall live and the weak shall die'*? Well, that mantra is true not just for a male's tadpoles, it is also true for a female's egg. I'm going to keep things nice and simple by giving you a broad brush approach to the reproduction department inside Sara.

We'll start at a woman's egg production department. The Ovaries.

Now don't ask me why the egg production department is called 'The Ovaries.' I don't know, so let's move on. I'm sure we will come across some more strange names appertaining to a woman's various reproductive parts, but just ignore them and accept that that's what they were named by some long dead educated person.

Anyway, Elsie, the egg production manager, has an office and an egg maker in Sara's Ovaries. There are, in fact, two Ovaries. They stand alone, quite a distance away from each other, so Elsie has to manage one of them with a sort of internet link via Brian's department.

Inside technology is wonderful, isn't it?

Elsie has a quiet and relaxed lifestyle because she doesn't have very much to do. Her one task in life is to make sure that one egg, and one egg only, is ready to leave the egg making department once every outside world twenty-eight day cycle.

Now, the egg's free passage from the egg production department is hindered by a sea of fluid. This is where the egg has to make a huge effort to swim and reach a platform, in egg terms a few miles away, at the top of a downward sloping tunnel called the Oviduct (Fallopian Tube), or egg transfer department. The egg has a little bit of help because there are finger-like extensions surrounding the expanded opening of the egg production department, like a series of piers reaching out into the sea from a sandy beach, but there is still a fair way for the egg to swim. It must be strong and healthy. Elsie makes sure that only the fittest of eggs leave her department, although she is not always successful with this. Stuff happens, you know.

Generally, the sea is relatively calm for the egg's swim. Sometimes, however, Sara decides to go for a jog around the block. This makes the sea really choppy with tall waves, further hindering any egg that might be swimming during Sara's jog, but sea currents help it on its way.

Anita, the Oviduct manager, patiently waits for the egg's arrival with a towel and some nourishment in a warm hut on the platform. Anita's job is to keep the staircase in the Fallopian Tube nice and clean and well lit for the egg to proceed in safety down to the egg hotel - what the outsiders call the Uterus. After a short rest the egg starts down the staircase, dreaming of things to come…

Okay. Sid's tadpoles have had a harrowing journey from Sid, and what remains of them, a few million, regroup in Sara's arrival lounge immediately after being shot out of Sid's inflated final exit chute. They rest up for a while taking in some nourishment before continuing their journey towards the arrival lounge exit to meet the egg somewhere in the Fallopian Tube, like a horde of people walking down the Mall to see the King on his balcony. The tadpoles have a long climb in front of them and one of them must pair with the egg within a couple of hours.

Off they go, jovially swapping anecdotes and laughing on their way up the staircase in the Fallopian Tube.

When the egg and the tadpoles meet it is wake-up time for the egg. She is surrounded by tadpoles, all pushing against her sides trying to find a weak spot and an easy way into her inner chamber. The egg has to fight hard to stop them all from entering while she chooses the fittest and most handsome tadpole to enter the inner chamber and pair with her. There are loads to choose from, all sporting their muscles and six-packs and showing off, like a bunch of blokes vying for the attention of a bunch of women in a dance hall... Just like a usual Saturday night out on the town.

Eventually, the egg grants entry to its inner chamber and a single tadpole grins and sticks two fingers up at the rest of the tadpoles as it enters the egg. It takes two to three days for the egg and tadpole to pair. The egg then finishes its stroll down the staircase. In about two weeks, outside world time, it is received by Eva, the Egg Hotel (aka Uterus) manager.

The Egg Hotel (aka Uterus) is just one room but it is a five star establishment. Every twenty-eight days (outside world time) Eva hoses down all the surfaces of this room and replaces its interior with a plush, soft, cushioned lining to receive the egg that has been sent down by Elsie. Most of the eggs that arrive have not been paired by a tadpole, so at the end of the outside world twenty-eight day cycle those unpaired eggs are flushed

103

out of Sara's egg hotel with the old, now not so plush surface liner. As soon as the room is spotlessly clean she repeats the cycle of installing a plush, soft, cushioned lining, ready for the next egg.

This is a never-ending task that is grossly underestimated and under-appreciated by the rest of Sara's tiny people. Eva, however, is proud of the job she does to support Sara, and she is always on time with her hosing down and cleaning.

*

Early one morning, Eva receives a memo from Elsie:

INTERNAL MEMO

From: Elsie/Egg production manager
To: Eva/Egg Hotel

Re: Advance notification

Hi Eva,
I've just received notification from Brian that Lee in listening has heard Sid and Sara talking about making a baby and Brian tells me that they coupled together last night.
Brian has asked me to ask you to make sure that the hotel is prepared and on stand-by for an egg paired by one of Sid's tadpoles.

Regards,
Elsie

Eva's curt reply is a classic example of how not to influence people and make friends:

INTERNAL MEMO

From: Eva/Egg Hotel
To: Elsie/Egg production manager
c.c.: Brian/Brain manager

Re: Advance notification

My department is ALWAYS ready to receive eggs, paired or not.
And Brian - If you've got a message for me don't send one of your lackies. Tell me yourself!

Eva.

It may be of interest to you that Brian and Eva once had a thing going between them, but Brian found the journey down to the Egg Hotel too time consuming, so he dumped Eva and made a bee-line for Lee…

Anyway, Eva makes a final inspection of the hotel and patiently waits for Sara's egg to arrive. When it appears from the Fallopian Tube, Eva greets it with some nourishment and shows it to its place on the wall of the plush, soft, cushioned lined room.

On the way she asks, "Have you paired with a tadpole?"

"Yeah. What a pairing! Sid's tadpole is really fit and handsome, You would pair with it yourself if you had the chance. Muscles like inflated balloons and a six-pack that looks like the base of an outside world bouncy castle. Boy! Did we have some fun after I'd let him in...!"

"Too much information," answered a bored Eva. "I only asked if you'd paired. I didn't want a blow-by-blow description."

"Oh dear... got out of the wrong side of the bed, have we?"

Eva ignored the egg's last remark and manipulated it further into the plush, soft, cushioned lining.

Turning on her heels, she made for her office with the words, "Sleep tight, divide lots, and I'll return in about nine months time to prepare for Sara's birth. Do you know if it will be a boy or a girl?"

"Nah, not yet, but I've got a feeling this is going to be a girl."

"Oh? What gives you that feeling?"

"I reckon she's gonna be like Sara... Gorgeous and intelligent."

And *THAT'S* how Suzy was made...

Chapter 17
(Cough, cough, cough)

The year, outside world time, is 2020. January 2020, to be precise. Any time now, all Hell is going to be let loose.

Sid's chesty elastic band never went away completely. It usually makes its presence known after a big meal but because it disappears after a while Sid just ignores it...

Tonight, Sid and Sara are sat in their local theatre instead of sitting in front of their TV.

The theatre puts on a film each month to give the audiences something other than a stage play to watch, and Sid booked tickets for Sara and himself for tonight's film because he recently read a good write-up about it. They both settled down in their seats and waited for the house lights to dim in advance of the big screen waking up and the speakers shouting out millions of decibels when the film starts.

Behind them is a Vomitorium. Behind that is another row of seats.

'Vomitorium?' I hear you ask. I can see you smirking and thinking that this is a description of something nasty but you're only halfway there. According to several accounts that I've read, a Vomitorium is a passage situated behind or below a tier of seats. The Latin word vomitorium, plural vomitoria, is derived from the verb 'to spew forth'. Vomitoria, in ancient Roman architecture, were designed to allow rapid egress for crowds in amphitheatres, but I bet you that they were used for something more useful after quaffing a few demijohns of wine...

Anyway, as soon as the house lights dimmed and the big screen flickered into life a woman, sat behind Sid, began to cough. Now, this cough wasn't a discrete, semi-silent cough that one tries to hide when in posh company. This cough was loud, and incessant, and unrelenting. The coughing went on throughout all of the film and it was abundantly obvious that the woman didn't have the courtesy to cover her mouth, because Sid felt a blast of air on the back of his head each time a cough was released from the woman's inconsiderate hole in the front of her face.

Sid turned, several times, to shoot a reproachful stare at the woman but she ignored his looks and sat, straight faced, watching the film as if Sid didn't exist. He even got a face full of cough during one of his turn-rounds. He was ready to explode about halfway through the film but Sara put a hand on his arm to stop him saying something to the woman that he might regret.

At the end of the film, when the credits were rolling upwards on the big screen, Sid felt the back of his neck and realised that it was wet. Not just wet, but saturated!

He stood, angrily, and turned to give the woman a piece of his mind, but she was gone. Following the line of people queuing on the Vomitorium to reach the exit door he saw her leaving the auditorium, still coughing, still not using her hand, or handkerchief, or even a sleeve to stifle the passage of spit projecting from her mouth.

Three days later, Sid and Sara began to cough.

Not just any cough. This cough, for them both, was incessant and unrelenting and kept them both awake for the whole of the night…

Chapter 18
(More oxygen)

Inside, Bella, the bellows (aka Lungs) manager, has found it necessary to disturb her neighbour, Piers the pump manager, from his busy schedule.

She fancies Piers no end and tries to find any excuse to talk to him, but Piers is oblivious to her charms. That's probably because she doesn't have any.

The name Bella originates from the Latin name 'Belle', meaning beauty. Bella is far from beautiful. In her spare time she enjoys pumping iron. The reason for this pastime is that it keeps her fit. This is probably only half true. Bella doesn't like to be pushed around by *anybody*, including Brian, the brain manager, so the inference I allude to is the fact that she is six feet six inches tall (in tiny people terms), equally as wide, and has muscles that can easily pull a steam train and four carriages. She is more than a match for anyone in an inside world arm wrestling competition.

They do play games inside, and arm wrestling is one of their favourite spectator sports. Bella always ends up as the champion - every time.

Another factor influencing whether she can get a full time boyfriend is her brusque manner. She doesn't suffer fools gladly, and she is the first to say so. She doesn't so much stand out in a crowd, it's more like she stands *in the middle* of a crowd, with a huge gap between her and everyone else, like a drop of oil on the surface of water. That's because most of the inside community are somewhat intimidated by her.

And she's loud. When she talks, people can feel the hair on their heads being swept backwards, as if in an outside real world gale.

Actually, her physique makes her the ideal choice for someone who manages the bellows. She sometimes needs to pump these by hand to give Sid's respiratory muscles, his Diaphragm and Intercostal muscles, an extra bit of help when Sid is exercising. Today, however, Sid is still in bed and trying to get some sleep to make up for the sleep he lost last night.

Unfortunately his cough will not permit any sleep. It has deteriorated during the night and Sid's life is one long bout of coughing. His respiratory muscles are crying out for some rest, but Sid's cough won't give them any.

"Piers? Are you there, Piers?" called Bella, from the doorway.

Piers got up from his terminal and thought to himself '*What does she want now?*'

"Hello, Bella. What can I do for you?"

Piers immediately regretted asking this question. He's asked it before and in between Bella's laugh that sounds like a horse in pain, she has made suggestive remarks about his spare time. This time, however, when he approached Bella he could see some concern in her face.

"What's wrong, Bella? You look a bit upset."

"I'm really worried about Sid, Piers. He's done nothing but cough all night. I've been pumping the bellows for hours, but even with his respiratory muscles working full pelt there is nothing I can do to increase the oxygen supply to his insides."

Piers saw tears beginning to form in Bella's eyes. Clearly, she is very upset. Piers has never seen her in this state before, and he now feels genuinely concerned about her.

"Have you reported it to Brian? You know he likes to be informed of stuff like this."

"Yes. He's promised to pay me a visit as soon as he has finished what he is doing, but I need to get more oxygen into Sid as soon as possible or everyone inside will suffer. I'm so tired, Piers, and I'm letting everyone down. I don't know what to do," sobbed Bella.

"You're not letting anyone down, Bella," sympathised Piers.

He tried to put an arm around her shoulders to comfort her, but couldn't quite reach all the way.

"Look, let me get a couple of my team to help you with the bellows, and I'll get onto Brian to do something pronto."

"Thank you, Piers. You're so sweet I could hug you to death…" Piers's feet left the ground as Bella hugged all the breath out of his own bellows.

"Can't… Breathe…" spluttered Piers, and Bella released her vice-like embrace.

"Oh, sorry."

Gasping for air, Piers instructed Bella, "Go back to your department and I'll send someone round."

Bella turned and hurried back to the bellows. Piers got straight on the phone to Brian. Someone in the brain department answered Brian's phone.

"Brain department."

"Is Brian there? I need to talk to him urgently."

"He's in, but he's a bit tied up at the moment. Can I help?"

"Not really. Bella, the bellows manager, needs an urgent visit from Brian. She's sent him a message, but not got any response yet. She really needs some help down here."

"Brian has seen Bella's message but he is fire-fighting a problem, right now. Something about the oxygen supply, I think."

"Oh. Right. Get a message to Brian to get down to the bellows department asap. I'll go and see if I can do anything to help Bella."

"Okay, will do."

Piers instructed his own 2IC to step up to the control terminal to take over from him while he goes to the Bellows department. The 2IC responded in a hurried tone.

"Brian's just sent an urgent memo to all departments. Do you want to see it before you go?"

Piers returned to his terminal and opened up his message box.

URGENT ACTION NOTE

From: Brian/brain manager
To: All departments
This message was sent with High importance.

VIRUS ALERT

A vicious virus has penetrated Sid's outer defences and has taken control of the bellows. The virus is intent on preventing Sid's system from distributing oxygen and the situation is now highly unstable. Sid's oxygen levels are reaching critical lows.

Daphne, send me a full report on how your immune department is coping.

Piers, let me know what the state of your Adrenalin reserve is. Sid may well need a sudden burst to cope with any pump problems brought on by the lack of oxygen.

Bella, I have received your message. I'll get down to your department as soon as I can. In the meantime, do you need any more manual assistance?

This situation is deteriorating very rapidly, people, so put your reserve staff on standby. They will probably be required in the very near future.

Brian.

Handing control of his department to his 2IC, Piers dashed over to the bellows department to help Bella.

Chapter 19
(The helpline)

Outside, the cough virus didn't affect Sara as badly as it affected Sid. Maybe her keep fit regime helped her immune system to fight it.

Sid's condition, however, deteriorated very rapidly. At first, he just had a slight fever and sore throat, with occasional chills. As the night changed to day it became increasingly more difficult for Sid to breathe. Laying in bed, semi-conscious, he became confused and unable to speak properly. Sara worried about Sid's wheezing and his inability to get a proper flow of air into his lungs. He constantly complained about the return of the elastic band around his chest. Sara tried to take his pulse count, but Sid's irregular heartbeat just gave Sara the feel of a ball bouncing around inside his wrist.

As the morning progressed to afternoon, Sara decided it was time to find out what to do about Sid's deteriorating condition. She decided to seek advice by dialling the NHS 111 phone number.

A call centre operative answered with a cheery "NHS Helpline. How can I help you?"

"My husband is in a bad way and finding it difficult to breathe."

"Is he conscious?"

"Yes, but it's difficult for him to speak."

"Okay. Can I start by taking your telephone number?"

Telephone number provided by Sara, the next question was, "And your address?"

Address provided by Sara, the next question was, "Which doctor's surgery do you normally attend?"

Name of surgery provided by Sara who was, by now becoming increasingly annoyed at the bureaucracy involved in getting advice.

"Please hold the line while I find a doctor for you…"

Before Sara could respond the telephone clicked and some tacky music was piped down the line to her. After about ninety seconds the NHS operator returned.

"It sounds as if your husband has got just a touch of the flu, but I've found a doctor that can see you immediately, Mrs. Smethers. I've made an appointment for you. Can you take your husband to the following address…?"

The address of the surgery was dictated to Sara, who was slightly put out by the advice she was given. "I'll try." Was all that she could say.

Sara had expected to be given specific advice about how to make Sid more comfortable. Instead, she got the address of a surgery that was about thirty miles away but there was no way that she would be able to get Sid out of bed, downstairs and into the car in the semi-conscious state that he was in.

As Sara cogitated how she could get Sid to the surgery the telephone chirped out a 'come and get me' request. Picking up the handset, Sara answered, "Hello?"

"Mrs. Smethers?"

"Yes, speaking."

"It's the NHS helpline here. We've just been told that the appointment at the surgery is unavailable. Can you call the 111 number back this evening to see if there are any other available appointments?"

Frustrated, Sara didn't give the NHS operator the courtesy of a reply. She ended the call by hanging up on the caller. Sid's constant coughing and wheezing worried her.

Sid wasn't all that perturbed by it because he was almost comatose…

Chapter 20
(A war)

We need to go back in time, briefly, to explain where Sid's cough originated.

On the thirty-first of December, 2019, less than one month before Sid's neck was showered with airborne spit from a woman sat behind him, the World Health Organisation (WHO) first learned of a new virus following a report of a cluster of cases of so-called viral pneumonia in Wuhan, China.

The newly discovered virus, caused by severe acute respiratory syndrome coronavirus 2 (SARS-Cov-2), was given the shorter name of COVID-19.

COVID-19 spread rapidly to become a world-wide pandemic. This pandemic ranked fifth in the list of deadliest epidemics and pandemics in history, topped only by HIV/AIDS (1981 to date), Bubonic Plague (541 - 549), Spanish Flu (1918 - 1920) and, top of the list, Black Death (1346 - 1353). In excess of seven hundred million known cases of Covid-19 have been reported, with more than six million deaths from this virus being confirmed.

For almost two years the whole world came to a virtual standstill as hospitals became overwhelmed by the number of cases brought to them. Ambulances queued outside the emergency admissions departments waiting for someone to come and get the patients desperately gasping for oxygen. Many patients were even treated in the ambulances because there was an acute lack of beds in the hospitals.

In the UK the pandemic became the order of the day for the UK government, with discussions centred on 'bed blocking' by elderly pensioners. Perversely, the so-called 'bed blockers' were discharged to care homes to make room for younger patients, thereby spreading the virus to other elderly care home residents. Consequently many of the relocated 'bed blockers' and, indeed, care home occupants died in care.

An acute shortage of bottled oxygen resulted in hospitals everywhere running out of reserve supplies.

Chaos ensued.

Governments throughout the world closed down places where people usually congregated - offices, pubs, theatres, factories, shops, supermarkets, etc. - and even introduced emergency laws to stop people congregating! Not that that stopped some government ministers from holding parties…

*

Return to January, 2020. Cut to Sid's insides.

It is now apparent that Sid had caught COVID-19.

To remind you about what is happening inside, Brian has been asked to go down to Sid's bellows department, but he is busy organising an emergency response to the virus that has taken control of the bellows, and Piers, the pump manager, has left his 2IC in charge of the pump and is dashing over to the bellows department with a couple of his staff to help Bella, the bellows manager.

Brian got on the phone to Daphne, the defence force manager. "Hi, Daphne. Have you been able to do anything to kill this virus? Sid is in a bad way 'cos he can't get enough oxygen into him for distribution."

"I've dispatched as many fighters (aka white blood cells) as I've got but the virus just keeps mutating. I'm afraid I can't stop this thing from harming Sid."

"Do what you can to get more fighters from Manny, the metabolism status manager, Daphne, and mobilise them as quickly as possible. I can't ask any more than that."

"I'll keep on it and let you know what's happening."

Call terminated, Brian turned to his 2IC.

"Have we heard how Bella is coping?"

"Not yet, boss, but I'm watching the terminals for any sign of a change in Sid's condition."

"Okay. Get onto Merv to see if he can help Sid in any way."

"Done that, sir…" Brian's 2IC is good. He's applied for a promotion, and may well get one, given his track record of using his initiative and taking charge. "Merv is going to suggest to Sid that he closes his eyes and tries to get some sleep. Apparently, sleep helps in situations like these."

"Well done. Can you take over for a bit while I go to the bellows department to see what the situation is down there?"

"Yes, sir, no problem. I've got control of the terminals," answered the 2IC, logging on to Sid's controlling terminal.

Now cut to the bellows department.

Piers has installed a lever into a bellows emergency pump slot and everyone is pumping furiously. Working a shift routine of thirty minutes on, thirty minutes off (outside world time) Bella's team, with the added workforce from Piers's department, are just about coping with Sid's oxygen demand. Brian's department has partially shut down some of Sid's internal departments to ensure that Sid's pump and brain departments are provided with any available oxygen that the bellows can distribute to them.

Brian arrived in the bellows department and watched the frenzy of activity, for a while, from the lift doors.

A resting worker noticed him and shouted "Brian in attendance!"

Several of the workers stopped pumping and stood to attention.

"GET BACK TO WORK," shouted Bella, anxious to keep the oxygen flowing. "You two…," waving a hand at a couple of resting workers, "…take over here." The two workers jumped up off the floor, from where they were resting, and ran to take over Pier's and Bella's pumps.

Piers and Bella greeted Brian.

Brian said "Looks like everything's under control here. Bella, can you show me what's happening inside the bellows?"

"Yes, of course," answered Bella, ushering Brian over to one of her terminals.

Pressing the enter key on her keypad, her screen lit up. Brian took a deep breath as he watched the war acting out inside the bellows.

A massive battle was taking place between the army of Covid fighters and Daphne's army of immune fighters. Dead and dying fighters were strewn everywhere. Just as Daphne's immune fighters appeared to be making headway, the Covid fighters mutated and fought back viciously, despatching millions of immune fighter in a great surge.

With a worried look on his face, Brian spoke to Piers and Bella. "I've asked Daphne if she can increase production of immune fighters but she is struggling as much as you, Bella."

"I understand, Brian. This virus is the worst one I've ever come across."

"That's true. I'll see if any of the other departments can send some more bodies down here to help out. You lot must be pretty tired."

"We are," answered Piers, looking back at the pumps.

Brian advised, "I've partially closed down some departments so there must be a few spare workers sitting around doing nothing. I'll send them here."

"Thanks," answered Bella, then she suddenly ran towards the bellows pumps shouting "DON'T DO THAT! DON'T DO THAT! It'll damage the bellows!"

A couple of workers were manning the same pump and were both furiously oscillating the pump lever to try to speed up the process. Hearing Bella's shouts they immediately stopped pumping.

Bella shouted, "Listen in, everyone." Pumpers continued their steady pumping and the resting workers all looked up to wait for Bella to speak. "We must pump in unison and we must pump with a steady intensity. The bellows are particularly fragile, right now, so we must be extremely careful how the oxygen is pumped until the bellows are able to return to automatic mode." She turned to an operative, standing in front of a bank of pressure gauges. "How's the pressure?"

"Stable, but some of the departments are requesting more oxygen. Shall I open the outlets a bit more?"

"Do it," answered Bella, "but do it slowly."

Bella turned round to see that Brian had disappeared from the department. She presumed that he had returned back upstairs to his own patch. She saw Piers on the phone.

"What? How much?" Piers was asking, looking wide-eyed.

Turning to Bella, he said, "I've got to go Bella. Pump's got a problem. I'll leave my blokes down here until I need them."

"Okay, Piers. I owe you for this, big time. I'll make sure you are repaid… Somehow."

Piers smiled and dashed for the lift.

*

Cut to the pump department.

Piers was greeted by his 2IC. "Hi, Piers. Thanks for returning."

"No probs. What's wrong? You sounded pretty worried over the phone."

"I am. You'd better see this for yourself."

The 2IC went to one of the terminals and pointed at the screen. This particular terminal monitored the regularity of Sid's Pump beat. The line chart displayed on the screen showed that the peaks and troughs of Sid's Pump beat were anything but regular.

"Looks like premature pump beats, or PVC's."

"What's happening?" asked the 2IC.

"If PVC's come from the bottom pump chamber they are called Ventricular Contractions. Basically they are extra beats generated by faulty electrical signals that are, generally, not too much of a concern. But unless we can stabilise the pump beat Sid's PVCs could trigger long lasting arrhythmia which, in turn, may lead to a stroke. Sid's pump is just not getting enough oxygen…"

Piers went over to the adrenal terminal and increased the amount of Adrenalin to Sid's pump.

"I hope my reserves are okay," he said, more to himself than to his 2IC.

"I checked those, myself, this morning. The Adrenaline store was eighty-five percent full," the 2IC offered.

"Well done. It should be okay, but we had better keep an eye on it."

It took a couple of minutes for Sid's pump beat to stabilise, but Piers and his 2IC continued their watch on it.

Once more, it seems, Sid had sidestepped a major heart catastrophe...

*

Outside, Sid was involuntarily confined to his bed for a week.

Sara considered telephoning for an ambulance several times during that week, but Sid's condition seemed to be stable, albeit serious. There was not much she could do to help Sid overcome the effects of Covid-19, but she also knew from the media reports that there was little use in asking for an ambulance. The emergency ambulance service was completely overrun with Covid cases and it was reported that none were available. The government even mobilised the army to assist with patient transfer to hospital - not that any of the ambulances could offload their patients at the hospitals. They just queued outside until a doctor could get out to treat the unfortunate patients in the back of the vehicles.

Sid and Sara were on their own with this thing, and Sid would have to ride it out, like many other outsiders that had incubated this insidious bug.

In a semi-comatose state he'd had nothing to eat or drink for about three days, but towards the end of the week he had improved sufficiently to take in some fluids - orange juice, mainly, but also many cups of tea.

During Sid's semi-conscious state his immune system, assisted by the bellows pumpers, eventually overpowered the Covid army and Sid's equilibrium began to return to normal.

It was a close call, but Sid had survived the worst pandemic since the Black Death in medieval times.

Chapter 21
(Blackhead alert!)

Let's jump to the year 2023.

You might recall that I told you we would return to Suzy. No? Well, I did. You couldn't have been listening at the time.

Suzy is fifteen years old and she spends a lot of time 'making her face up' so that she looks fabulous for all the boys, especially Stan, her current beau.

Peering into a small, round mirror perched on her dressing table she suddenly stopped wafting her cheeks with the make-up brush and moved her face towards the mirror to get a close-up view of her forehead. She suddenly let out a piercing scream that startled the whole neighbourhood and prompted a busy-body three doors down to call the police. A chap out in his front garden, hoeing out his weeds, dropped his hoe and dashed across the road to see if anybody in Sid's house needed help.

Sid was out at the time but Sara dashed upstairs from the kitchen to see what had happened to Suzy. Opening Suzy's bedroom door she saw Suzy sat in front of her dressing table, sobbing.

"What's the matter, darling? Have you injured yourself? Are you in pain? What is it?"

"I've got a blackhead…!" arms outstretched, hands with their palms facing her head, fingers spread in horror.

"What? A blackhead?"

"Yes, a blackhead. A big one. What shall I do with it? I can't let Stan see me in this state!"

"What state? There's nothing wrong with you."

"Mum, you're not listening. I'VE GOT A BLACKHEAD!"

Sara took a deep breath and looked up at the ceiling, as if there was a suitable response written on it. She couldn't believe the drama that Suzy was making.

"What do I do about it, mum?" cried Suzy.

As composed as she could possibly be, Sara answered, "One blackhead isn't the end of the world. Just give it a squeeze and it'll be gone."

"But it'll leave a hole in my skin. You know how Stan likes to kiss my forehead. He won't come anywhere near me if he sees THIS!" pointing to the blackhead.

"Well, just cover it with some make-up. Then he won't see it. I'll get some cream from the chemist to make the blackhead go away."

"Now you're telling me NOT to squeeze it, but to leave it alone. I'll be the class's laughing stock."

"No, you won't," Sara lied, knowing how kids of Suzy's age, especially girls, jump on the slightest thing to make somebody's life, usually another girl, sheer purgatory. Suzy will have to put a pillowcase over her head each time she goes to school. That will be infinitely better than having the other girls in her class homing in on the blackhead.

Before Suzy could put some more drama queen into her performance, Sara was saved by the doorbell.

Leaving Suzy to brood over her blackhead, Sara went back downstairs and opened the door to see Seth, her gardening neighbour standing there.

"Is everything okay? I just heard Suzy scream," asked a concerned looking Seth.

"Everything is fine, Seth. She's just found a blackhead on her face, that's all."

"Oh dear. That's bad news…" replied Seth with a less than sympathetic smile on his face. "As I remember it, my Samantha had exactly the same reaction to her blackhead."

"Kids…" proffered Sara.

"Phuh! Yeah, kids…" with a jerk of Seth's head.

Seth did an about turn to head back to his weeding. Sara started back upstairs to see if she could pacify Suzy. No chance.

About fifteen minutes later Sid arrived back home from where he had been.

Opening the front door he shouted "I'm home."

Sara was, by now, in the kitchen. She went to the doorway to greet Sid as he walked down the hallway.

"How's Suzy?" asked Sid, always interested in his daughter's welfare.

"She's upstairs sulking about a tiny little blackhead on her face."

"Oh, really? I'll leave her to it, then. Has something happened at Selena's house? There's a police car parked outside it."

"No idea. I've not been outside this afternoon."

"Oh well. I'm sure Selena will tell us about it some time. She's not backward in coming forward with some gossip, is she?"

"Did you pick up my dry cleaning?" asked Sara.

"Yeah, left it in the car. I'll go and get it."

Sid went back outside to retrieve the dry cleaning and saw a policeman talking to Seth in the front of Seth's garden. As Sid opened his car door he noticed the policeman look skyward, nod, then turn his head to face Sid. Sid watched him return to his police car, occasionally looking back at Sid in an accusatory manner.

Returning to his home, Sid handed the dry cleaning to Sara. "Looks like Seth's just had the third degree from the police. They've gone, now."

Sid made a mental note to go talk to Suzy in a while to see if there was anything he could do to pacify her angst.

Chapter 22
(Closed Comedones)

Here's something I should remind you about; everybody... You, me, your friends, your relatives, your neighbours, everybody you know - literally everybody - has a community of really, really tiny people inside them. Men, women, everybody. What's more, the really, really tiny people inside everyone all have identical names. We've all got a Brian, the brain manager, and a Mick, the Masher, and a Kevin, the Kitchen manager, and everyone else I've previously mentioned.

They can't communicate with any outside people, or even with the really, really tiny people inside other outside people, but they do know what the outside people are doing because your Lee, in lookout, can see them and your Lee, in listening, can hear them. So don't go getting confused if I talk about them. Is that clear enough?

Good. I thought I would clarify that point before any of you start scratching your heads in puzzlement when I refer to the tiny people by name.

Outside, time flies... It is now 2024.

Suzy is now sixteen years old and her single blackhead has, unfortunately, developed into full blown Acne.

I'm jumping ahead of myself, slightly, so let's go back in time and see how Suzy practically encouraged her Acne by making herself attractive to the boys, Stan in particular.

The tiny people inside you need a lot of protection from germs. They also need something to keep all your body parts together. Without your skin for example, you would have to walk around holding your intestines, known as the waste chute by the tiny people, in your cupped hands in front of you... Yuk! - and not very convenient. The tiny people also require their dwelling temperature to be regulated.

So when The Almighty invented evolution He, or She, invented skin. The tiny people call your skin the 'big wrapping'.

Millions of years ago (outside world real time) when bacteria, measuring less than a thousandth of a millimetre in diameter, eventually evolved into animals something had to be added to the Big Wrapping to alert an animal to any sinister creature that may be crawling on its skin. Further, with a long, cold winter on its way the animals needed something to keep them warm. Bear in mind that quilted puffer coats, or parkas or duffle coats had not yet been thought of, so The Almighty invented hair that grows out of follicles within the layers of the Big Wrapping.

Okay, back to 2024.

Inside, the tiny people in Suzy are having a management meeting.

Brian settled them down to begin the meeting. "Okay, folks. Settle down quickly. I've got a busy day ahead, so I want this meeting over with as soon as possible."

Nods of approval - not every manager likes attending these meetings. Sometimes they can be tedious and boring.

Brian spoke to his 2IC. "Please read the minutes of the last meeting."

Minutes read, Brian asked, "Any questions?"

No response.

"Good. Merv, how much spare capacity have you got in Suzy's ideas chip. I may need to pass on a few suggestions to her after this meeting."

"Plenty," answered Merv, the message wires manager.

"Right. Now, Billy, the big wrapping manager, has sent me an email asking for some floor time. Is he here?"

Billy, the big wrapping manager, stood up to make his presence known and he was invited down to the front by Brian.

"The floor is yours," prompted Brian.

"Well," started Billy, "I've got a couple of items that concern me presently. One is about Suzy, the other relates to Sid. How much time have we got, Brian?"

"Don't write a book, Billy. Just give us the facts. Start with Suzy."

"Okay. Well, several months ago Suzy got a blackhead. Now, this is normal for some girls of her age, but she persisted in scrubbing it with a flannel. All this did was to block her follicles with bits of surface wrapping. To make matters worse, she used oil-based makeup which combined with the bits of wrapping to clog not just the blackhead pore but lots of others on her forehead. The pores have turned into Closed Comedones, or 'whiteheads' as the outsiders refer to them. Suzy makes matters worse by trying to cover the whiteheads with more makeup. Her wrapping can't breathe and expand properly with all that stuff covering it."

A woman in the group raised her hand for attention.

"Is it possible that her hormones could be interfering?"

"Absolutely," answered Billy, "I'm sure that her hormones may well be having some adverse effects, but all girls have a 'hormone problem'," dipping two fingers of both hands in the air, "especially when it's time for Eva to hose out the egg hotel. Many don't have this clogged pore problem, though. I think the outsiders refer to it as 'Acne'."

Brian joined the conversation.

"Lee, you've got some input on this, haven't you?"

Lee, from lookout (not to be confused with Lee, from listening) opened a file on his lap and looked through the papers.

"Yes, Suzy has been on the internet to find out why she's got this problem. It seems, from the stuff she read, that clogged pores create the right conditions for bacteria that normally live on the big wrapping to thrive. Sara's defence force system, apparently, then attacks the bacteria, causing the pain and swelling of a white pimple."

Daphne, the defence force manager, joined in. "Yes. I'm having quite a battle trying to eradicate the bacteria. I'm sure we all remember the hard job we had in disposing of those awful bacteria louts when Suzy got a dose of the Tangier trots."

There was lots of head nodding and private, face-to-face discussions in response to this comment.

"Settle down, everyone," interjected Brian, "We've got lots to get through. Does anyone have any suggestions that I can use?"

Lee from lookout stood up, once more. "Some papers that Suzy has read suggest that drugs the outsiders call Retinoids are effective in treating Acne, but there are side effects. Other research also suggests that a compound, called Cathelicidin, also eradicates bacteria, and there is some suggestion that Oxytetracycline might help with Daphne's defence force programme."

Brian thought about that comment for a moment, then brought this particular discussion to a halt.

"Sounds a bit too technical for us. We need some help with this. Merv, send a text to Suzy's ideas chip to prompt her to go see an educated person (aka doctor). Perhaps an educated person will come up with a suitable solution."

"Will do," replied Merv.

"Okay, next item on the agenda. Billy, you said something about Sid. The floor is yours, but be quick about it."

Billy ascended from his chair again. "Yeah. I was having a chat with Lee in lookout, the other day, and he mentioned something that rang bells with me. Apparently, Sid and Suzy recently visited an outsider's tourist place called St. Paul's Cathedral."

Several tiny people in the audience looked at each other and there were lots of mumblings.

"Aww…"

"Lovely…"

"That's nice…"

Brian interrupted the interruptions. "Quiet! Pay attention. This could be important. *Is* it important, Billy?"

Billy answered, "Perhaps Lee from lookout can answer that…?" sitting down.

Brian turned to Lee. "Lee, is it important?"

"Could be, Brian. Inside this tourist place is a huge open space covered by a dome, and you can actually get to the top of the dome, where there is a balcony to look out over the city."

"So?"

"Well, to get to this balcony there is a total of five hundred and twenty-eight steps to climb. Sid and Suzy did the lot. When they eventually arrived on the balcony Suzy noticed that Sid was wheezing, breathing *very* heavily and rubbing the top of his chest to the left of centre. He told Suzy that his chest felt like it was being squeezed by an

133

elastic band. Suzy was really concerned, at the time, 'cos Sid's face looked colourless and he had to rest for, maybe, ten minutes before he felt well enough to return to ground level. I watched all this."

Piers, Suzy's pump manager, jumped to his feet and said, "I remember that time. I had a hell of a job calming Suzy's pump down after that climb. I dread to think of what Sid's pump manager had to put up with, given Sid's age."

With a bit of anger in Brian's voice, he said, "Why wasn't I told about this, at the time?" looking accusingly at Piers and Lee.

They both looked down in embarrassment.

Brian asked, "Is Sid alright now?" staring at Piers, brow furrowed.

"Well, yes. I understand that there is a small amount of irregular pump beat, but he's apparently had this before. I got this info from Lee, Suzy's listening manager, after she heard Sid talking about it. It seems to correct itself after a while."

"Listen folks," said Brian, "I need to be told about this kind of incident the moment it happens. I can't do anything to get Suzy to help Sid if I don't know so *please...* tell someone in my department straight away. Got that?"

No response from the crowd.

"GOT THAT?" repeated Brian.

This time there were lots of 'yes sirs' and 'okays'.

"Right. Meeting over. You've all got my memo about Staff meeting dates. Don't be late."

From the discussion about Sid, at the staff meeting, it sounds very much like Sid may have a heart problem...

134

Chapter 23
(Party time)

Do you know that an average person has about six litres, or ten and a half pints, of blood being pumped around the body by the heart using a two-way plumbing system the outsiders call blood vessels (aka nourishment tubes).

Important stuff, blood (aka nourishment). It carries oxygen and nutrients, via arteries, to all your body's organs and tissues, and returns the deoxygenated blood back to the heart through veins. Some of the really, really tiny people inside you have a lot of work to get through to ensure that your nourishment is fit for purpose.

Here's a simple overview of the passage of nourishment travelling through the nourishment tubes:

From the heart (aka pump, managed by Piers), it is pumped down to Manny, the metabolism status (aka Liver) manager, to have all the harmful substances filtered out. This includes alcohol. Actually, this description of the liver's function is somewhat simplistic. At any given moment the liver holds about thirteen percent of the body's blood supply. That's about a pint of the stuff, and there are more than five hundred vital functions that have been identified with the liver.

Inside you, Manny, the metabolism status manager, is a busy person. His team's many tasks include clearing the blood of harmful substances, dead bacteria bugs that have been swept up after a war, and ensuring that Daphne, the defence force manager, is provided with an ample supply of immune fighters when they are required.

After the liver has broken down and extracted much of the harmful stuff, the by-products of filtration, including alcohol, are excreted into either the Intestine (aka waste chute) or back into the nourishment tubes for transportation to the Kidneys (aka filters).

Fay, the filters (aka Kidneys) manager, filters out the by-products excreted by the liver, including alcohol, and the waste product, in the form of urine, is then sent to the bladder (aka the tank) for storage. When the tank is almost full, the waste is expelled from the body via the final exit chute.

Most men know that it is extremely difficult to expel waste (aka have a wee-wee) if the final exit chute is inflated! So men always try to wait until the final exit chute is deflated before having a wee-wee.

Anyway, the filtered nourishment is finally pumped up to Bella to be re-oxygenated and distributed around the body once more.

Simple, isn't it?

Manny and Fay are engaged to be married, but they haven't set a date, yet, because Brian hasn't approved it. They were meant to have had an interview with Brian some time ago, but the Covid war broke out and Brian has been busy, to say the least. Manny has it on his 'To Do' list to remind Brian about the interview and arrange another meeting date.

*

Outside, Sid's brother, Scott, is getting married to Symone, Scott's long-time fiancé.

They met on a usual Saturday night on the town, before Scott got drunk and started to annoy everyone by singing out of tune loudly, and falling down.

The marriage has been in the planning stage for about twelve months now, and Sid was asked, early on, if he would be Scott's best man. Sid, naturally, accepted the invitation.

Inside, coincidentally, Manny and Fay, the Filters manager, eventually managed to get an interview with Brian who gave their engagement his blessing, and they decided to get married on the same day as Scott and Symone.

So when the wedding invitations were sent to the outsiders by Symone, Fay followed suit to the insiders. So there is going to be one hell of a big party, both outside and inside!

Outside, Sean, Symone's father, booked a village hall at the back of a pub for the reception. He did a fantastic deal with the pub landlord for supply of the food, wedding booze and waiters.

Inside, Brian's wedding gift to the couple was the setting up of a party room on top of Sid's right Liver lobe, in between Manny's office on top of the left Liver lobe and just a short hop from Fay's office atop the right filter.

During the process of helping to arrange Manny's marriage his 2IC sent a memo to Brian:

INTERNAL MEMO
Private & Confidential

From: Manny's 2IC
To: Brian/brain manager

Re: Manny's wedding to Fay.

Sir,
I am helping with the above wedding arrangements.

With your approval, I would like to divert some of the dizzy juice in Sid's nourishment into the many containers stored next to Manny's office. I think this would help to make the party go with a swing. Also, I wondered if you could send a message to Merv, the message wires manager, to encourage Sid to drink lots on the night so that we will have a plentiful supply of dizzy juice.

Your valued thoughts and comments on this matter will be gratefully appreciated.

I remain, sir, your faithful servant,
Manny's 2IC.

Brian's response:

INTERNAL MEMO
Private & Confidential

From: Brian/brain manager
To: Manny's 2IC

Re: Manny's wedding to Fay.

Yes, and yes.

Brian.

On receiving approval for his plan, Manny's 2IC got together with Fay's 2IC to discuss diverting some of the dizzy juice (aka alcohol) in Sid's nourishment (aka blood), into the many containers stored next to Manny's office before it reached the filters (aka Kidneys). These containers are stored in case of a leaky nourishment tube somewhere.

This was to be the insider's booze.

*

Outside, the day that everyone had been waiting for arrived.

Marriage ceremonies over, embarrassing car ride to the reception venue over (inside, Manny and Fay walked) meals over, speeches over and trips to the toilet over, it is now time to get down to some serious dancing and, of course, some serious drinking.

Sid left Sara to circulate while he propped up the bar.

Scott joined him after the mandatory first dance with his new wife.

"Hiya. Thanks for helping out with the cost, Sid."

"No problem, bro'. Symone's dad did a good job arranging this lot," replied Sid, waving his hand around.

"Yeah. He's a good bloke."

Sid's ideas chip suddenly fired up, in response to Merv's instruction from Brian. "Why are we stood here talking when everyone is enjoying themselves? Let's get legless!"

"You can, if you like," replied Scott. "I've got to stay reasonably sober to… Well… You know," shrugging his shoulders.

"Oh, yeah. I'll get a couple of the guys to join me while the women dance around their handbags."

"Good idea. I'll have a quick couple, then leave you to it."

Chapter 24
(Dizzy juice)

Here's a bit of useful information that you might like to keep.

Blood alcohol levels may be given in different ways, including the percentage of blood alcohol content (BAC). Typical results are:

- **Sober** (0.0% BAC). It's okay to drive your car.
- **Legally Intoxicated** (0.08% BAC). Best to give your car keys to someone else *before* you exceed the 0.0% cap.
- **Very Impaired** (0.08 - 0.40% BAC). At this blood alcohol level, you may have difficulty walking and speaking. Other symptoms may include confusion, nausea and drowsiness. A stupid question, but have any of you ever reached this level?
- **At Risk for serious complications** (Above 0.40% BAC). At this blood alcohol level you may be at risk for coma or even death! I'll bet that some of you have managed to briefly reach the coma stage.

So, if you drink alcohol faster than your liver can break it down, and the alcohol level in your blood reaches 0.08% or above… You're drunk.

Now, if you've been there you'll know that alcohol, in any proportion, interferes with the brain's communication pathways. It makes it harder for the brain to control balance, memory, speech and judgement.

Average Sid is no exception to this, and because he rarely drinks alcohol the effects on him, compared to a regular drinker, tend to be... What shall we say?... Exaggerated.

Scott, after a few dances... Actually, he was no better at dancing than the bar propper-uppers... Scott decided that Symone's toes needed a rest from his size twelves and he had decided to join the lad's group at about ten forty-five.

At about eleven-fifty (outside world time) several of the guests had left, but many more continued to party, drink booze, go to the toilets, come back from the toilets, drink some more booze and continue to party. Sid and a few of the blokes - those that couldn't dance - had propped up the bar all night, their drinks glasses being replenished with a never-ending supply of booze.

Including Sid, this lad's group numbered six. Present were Stan, Suzy's boyfriend, Sean, Symone's father, Steve, Stan's dad, Scott and Spencer. Remember Spencer... Sara's previous boyfriend? Perhaps I should expand, a little, on Spencer's background.

Sid, Scott, Sara and Spencer were all at school together. Sid and Spencer were good pals. They went to the football matches together when the local team played at home, they spent time at the weekends together and they did their homework together.

In their final year - the year that most boys and most girls explore each other's bodies in more detail - Sara threw herself at Spencer. Now, Sid fancied Sara as much as any bloke in the school. Even at that age she was gorgeous, and every boy's wet dream, but average Sid was too shy to approach Sara for a date, so he accepted that Spencer was the chosen one and got on with his life.

In actual fact, Sara wanted Sid to ask her for a date because she fancied *him* and not Spencer. God knows why she was attracted to Sid 'cos they were opposite in every way possible.

The idea of throwing herself at Spencer was intended to make Sid jealous, with average Sid possibly being fired into some sort of action, but it didn't work, did it? Sid was just too average or, perhaps naive, to pick up on the vibes from Sara.

So Sara and Spencer knocked around for several weeks and Sid was left to go the football matches on his own. On the few occasions when Sid and Spencer did get together, usually to do their homework, Spencer was full of what he and Sara had done, when they did it, where they did it and how long they did it for.

"I'm the luckiest bloke alive," boasted Spencer. "All the guys at school fancy her, but she picked me, of all people."

"Yeah," replied Sid, bored by Spencer's crowing about his conquests with Sara.

"Come on, Sid. Don't tell me you don't fancy her."

"Maybe."

"There's no maybe about it, is there? You fancy her as much as any of the other blokes in school, don't you? Admit it."

"Well… yes I do, but I don't go around bragging about it."

Spencer detected some animosity in Sid's reply so he quickly changed the subject.

It turns out that Spencer mentioned this conversation to Sara, who realised her mistake and quickly dumped Spencer to throw herself at Sid. That worked. Sid and Sara then got together, married and had Suzy.

There were absolutely no ill feelings, at the time, about Sara's switch in loyalties from Spencer to Sid, hence Spencer's attendance at the wedding and reception with his own wife and daughter. The two men had remained friends all their lives... until the night of Scott's wedding.

Cut back to the outsider's wedding reception.

The lad's group is now well on the way to a 0.40% BAC.

Sara and Symone, arm-in-arm, barged in on the lad's group.

Sara asked "Haven't you lot had enough to drink?"

Stan replied "Nope," to chuckles throughout the lad's group.

Symone turned to Scott. "Well make sure you're in a fit state to take me upstairs," a suggestive smile on her face.

Scott replied, drunkenly, "I'll take you down here, if you're that eager!" Howls of laughter all round.

The girls knew that they were on a loser with this group, so they went back to their table for some more chat and some more booze.

The lads continued to chat and replenish their drinks glasses, and by twelve-thirty the dizzy juice was definitely hovering just under the 0.40% BAC. Their eyes were half closed and their eyeballs looked like two tomatoes. Like marionette puppets, their heads swayed from back-to-front and round-and-round on top of their necks - especially when they talked - and their knees had a habit of jerking forward without permission. The conversation spiralled into asinine sentences.

Scott to Sid - "I love you, bro'," stabbing a finger into Sid's chest.

Sid to Scott - "I love you, too, bro'," drilling his own finger into Scott's chest.

Scott, turning to the rest of the lads - "And I love you, Stan," more finger drilling, "and you, Sean," another finger stab, "and I love you, Steve," this time his finger missed Steve's left arm, "and I love you, Spencer," finger pointing skywards as Scott fell backwards onto the edge of the bar, head trying to find a place to balance.

The finger stabbing suddenly became the order of the night as everyone in the lad's group drilled their fingers into each other's chest continually, repeating "...and I love you," with each stab.

Suddenly, an ominous silence descended on the group when Spencer loudly declared "And I love Sara..." The lad's all seemed to sober up as they looked at Sid and waited for his response.

"Too bad you lost her," retorted Sid.

"Yeah, but I had a good time with her at school before you took her from me."

The silence now turned into a dark cloud. The guys looked round at each other, waiting for something to happen.

"For a start, I didn't take her, she dumped you to come to me voluntarily. And you didn't touch her. She told me that she'd had enough of your pawing at her so she stopped you every time you tried to grope her, and she was sick of you bragging about your 'achievements' with Symone."

With that, there was a chorus of "Whoa..." from the lads.

Spencer had to get the last word in, didn't he?

145

"Tell you what, Sid. Symone was better at it than Sara!"

They were the last words that Spencer spoke, that night.

*

Cut to the Sid's inside world.

Fay and Manny's party is going full swing. Brian and Lee, from listening, had disappeared somewhere, no doubt to 'discuss' something - probably not work related. Manny's 2IC and Fay's 2IC decided to cultivate their new-found friendship by sitting in a corner and staring into each other's eyes, and the rest of the crowd partied and enjoyed the evening.

Bella's 2IC dashed into the party room, looking worried. He had volunteered to be on the skeleton staff to keep the inside systems running smoothly.

Bella stood up from her table of women chatting away and having a good time gossiping about the men, and went to her 2IC, who was stood just inside the door looking round the room for her.

"Everything okay?" she asked.

"There's a problem with the outsiders."

"Oh? What?"

"They've had too much dizzy juice and they've stopped enjoying themselves."

"What are they doing?"

"Well, the outside men are arguing and the outside women have stopped dancing and have gone to join the men."

"Have you been up to the brain department to find out the status of Sid's systems?"

"Yes. I went there on my way here. Merv's 2IC is worried about Sid's balance, his communication pathways and his speech. His memory chips are all deleting information... Sid's overall judgement has been impaired by the dizzy juice. Also, Max's 2IC is concerned about the stability of Sid's two supporting stanchions."

Max, the mechanics (aka Skeleton) manager, looks after a person's mechanical components (aka Bones) and you may have already guessed that Sid's 'supporting mechanics' are his legs.

Bella thought for a moment then issued her orders to her 2IC. "Get back to your station and keep me informed of events." She turned round and shouted "Does anyone know where Brian is?"

Someone piped up, "Probably in the Cochlea Labyrinth discussing something with Lee."

Laughs all round.

Eva, the egg hotel manager, huffed and puffed a bit and muttered something uncomplimentary about Lee under her breath. You may recall that she and Brian once had something between them until Brian chased after Lee...

The room descended into silence.

Bella took the bull by the horns and suggested, "It's time to pack up, folks. It sounds like Sid might need a bit of help soon and I think we should be ready, just in case..."

She was unable to finish her sentence.

The room shook as if an earthquake had struck. The tiny people fell off their chairs, tables were upturned, food spilled onto the floor and booze spread over the carpet like a collapsed dam.

Then the room slowly turned on its side, depositing everyone against a wall. A nourishment tube split and nourishment spurted out, spraying the ceiling and walls with sticky nutrition.

Now, you may wonder why this doesn't happen when Sid lays down on his pillow to go to sleep. Well, It is clear that the spinning of the gyroscopes that keep all departments upright, even during sleep, have been interrupted by something that has happened outside, and some of them slowed to a standstill while others stopped completely and toppled over.

Up in the brain department chaos ensued. Some of the strip lighting had collapsed from the ceiling and the neon tubes had exploded. Tables, chairs and PC's were strewn around with tiny people lying down, tangled up in the terminal cables. One-by-one, the terminals blinked off as the brain servers shut down, plunging the room into darkness.

The lookout department fared no better, the lookouts having been unceremoniously tipped from their seats. They, too, were plunged into darkness as the brain servers shut down and Sid's eyelids (aka shades) automatically closed and locked into place.

In the Cochlea Labyrinth Brian and Lee were suddenly thrown to the floor before this place, also, turned on its side, depositing them against a Labyrinth wall.

The microphones in the listening department got vibrated from the stands. The listening department operatives got squashed up against a wall by the PC desks.

Every department had experienced the earthquake followed by a ninety degree rotation. Then there was a sudden crash and everything, and everyone inside their department rooms, got bounced into the air. They landed in a heap amongst the chaos of tables, chairs, food, booze, PC's, terminals and cabling. Alarm sirens and bells shouted out in every department and red lights flashed above every exit.

Everyone sat up and looked around, dazed by the violence that had just spoiled their inside party and their inside workplaces. Some of the tiny people held their bloody heads in their hands, others cradled their arms or legs. Some just laid where they had dropped, unconscious.

What had caused such chaos and injured the tiny people inside?

*

Let's return to the outside and cut back to the point where Sid and Spencer were racking up each other's intoxicated emotions.

"Tell you what, Sid. Symone was better at it than Sara!"

Scott didn't wait for Sid to respond. He whacked Spencer on the side of his head.

"NOBODY talks about my wife like that!" he spat.

Spencer's lights went out and he stiffly rotated backwards on his heels, like a plank that someone had let go of.

The ladies had all joined the lads as soon as the 'discussion' between Sid and Spencer got loud and heated. The whole room was blanketed in silence when Scott dropped Spencer.

Sandra, Spencer's wife, let fly with a hefty slap to Scott's left cheek. Now, this was a cue for Symone to join in with a right hook to Sandra's jaw, so one of the other wives - a close friend of Sandra - started throwing badly aimed punches at Symone.

This 'lad's discussion' was getting out of hand.

One of the lads pushed Sandra's attacker in the chest to stop her flaying her fists at Symone, so this became a cue for one of the other lads to hurtle into this guy, all guns firing.

The place descended into one big boxing ring with the lads fighting each other, the ladies swinging their handbags at each other and even the children rolling around in a mass wrangle.

In the carnage that had developed, Sid was pushed backwards and the back of his head hit the bar. Stunned, he plopped onto the floor (that was the earthquake that the insiders felt - the one that interrupted the gyroscopes) and then he slid sideways across the front of the bar (the inside ninety degree rotation) until he came to a final resting place by slumping onto his side (the insiders big bounce).

You may think that the bang on his head against the bar, coupled with the effects of the dizzy juice, had made Sid unconscious. You would be wrong. In actual fact, the jolt to the PC servers in his brain department, as a consequence of the bang to his head, caused unforced shut-downs of the PC's. With no PC's to control his systems, Sid became unconscious.

In this state he didn't feel the elastic band tighten around his chest, or the uneven beat of his heart…

Both parties, by all accounts, were definitely smash hits…

Chapter 25
(The party's over - Nat King Cole, 1957)

Outside, everyone has recovered from the smash hit wedding receptions.

It took a while, but hangovers have gone, black eyes are now a sort of purple red rings around the eye socket, noses still have a re-aligning plaster across the nose bridge and loose teeth have re-seated themselves so that the owners can now bite into an apple.

Lots of phone calls were made, by the wedding guests to each other, all agreeing what a fantastic time they had had, how much they enjoyed the meal and how they envied the bride's dress... Before it got torn.

Inexplicably, everyone is still good buddies, despite the drunken brawl that forced the pub landlord to close the venue down. He became aware of the brawl when a woman entered the bar asking where the toilets were so that she could clean the blood from her bent nose.

"What the hell happened to you?" he asked.

"Everybody's fighting," she replied.

The landlord walked from behind the bar and went outside to make his way to the reception hall. On the way he circumnavigated a couple of blokes rolling around in the gravel yard in a drunken pretence at fighting. Inside the building, he found pandemonium. Tables were upturned, chairs were strewn around and most of the guests were lashing out at each other, the women in one corner, the men next to the bar, and the children in the hallway.

Ducking down to avoid a plate of chicken bones that had been thrown, by someone at someone, he went to the stage, took the microphone from the lead guitarist who, ironically, was still singing Whitney Houston's *'I will always love you"*, and he bellowed, "CAN I HAVE EVERYONE'S ATTENTION, PLEASE?"

Silence descended on the crowd as they ceased to fight. Everyone turned to face the stage.

"I'm sorry to have to break up your party but I must now shut the bar and lock up the pub. You're welcome to stay here, if you wish, but I suggest you all go home... soon."

The band started to play that eternal song *'The party's over'*, an oldie, sung by Nat King Cole in 1957.

So everyone dusted themselves down, picked up the ones that were lying around, hugged each other and left with those immortal words, "Keep in touch," or, "We'll have to get together again, sometime," or, "Call me."

Sometimes, people can be the antithesis of how they appear...

*

Anyway, inside, while Sid was horizontal in front of the bar Brian managed to get a PC re-booted and up-and-running, and he sent a message to Merv, the message wires manager;

INTERNAL MEMO
From: Brian/brain manager
To: Merv/message wires manager
Re : Departmental Cleanup

Merv,
Please send a spark to Sid's ideas chip to get him to take it easy while we put a cleanup operation into action.

Brian.

*

Outside, when all the guests had departed from the reception hall, Sid was poured into a taxi by Scott and Sara.

During the afternoon of the following day he was laid on the couch, nursing a bump on the back of his head. He didn't remember anything about the brawl, or how he got home after the reception. He wasn't sure if the bump on the back of his head was giving him a thumping headache, or if it was the hangover from the reception booze. Either way, the 'idea' that Merv had sent to his ideas chip told him to have a sleep for an hour or two.

The insiders faced many hours of cleaning up, repairing equipment and patching up the injured.

Sid didn't wake up until it was time to go to bed. Perhaps he will feel better tomorrow...

*

Piers thanked Merv for his ideas chip command. Piers was beginning to worry about Sid's pump and he breathed a sigh of relief when Sid closed his eyes, once more, and went to sleep for the night.

Piers would use this time to carry out a detailed inspection of Sid's pump...

Chapter 26
(Forgotten anything?)

September, 2026.

Sid and Sara have just taken Suzy to the campus accommodation at her chosen university.

Suzy is now eighteen years old and it is her first time away from home. She is looking forward to university life and all that goes with it - lots of learning, lots of booze, and… Boys. Lots of boys. No, she hasn't broken up with Stan. It's just that Suzy's university doesn't provide the subjects that Stan wanted, so, unfortunately, he was taken to a different university by Steve and Stella, his parents.

Suzy and Stan have promised to keep in touch and to spend their holiday periods together, but Suzy is still looking forward to meeting all those boys. It goes without saying that Stan, likewise, is looking forward to meeting all those girls…

Having deposited Suzy in her accommodation, unloaded the vast volume of stuff that freshers need for their campus apartment and left her to get to know her new neighbours, Sid drove back home. Sitting in the lounge with a cup of tea, Sara retrieved the holiday brochures from their hiding place and sat next to Sid to start planning a Christmas holiday.

"Now that Suzy is out of the nest, what about a Christmas holiday? I'm sure we can get a spare room, somewhere," suggested Sara.

"Great, I'm in. Any ideas?"

"D'you fancy Morrocco, again? It's nice and sunny and the water is usually quite warm," answered Sara, flicking through a brochure.

"No way! Not after Tangiers. What about Cyprus?"

"Nah. The water's too shallow. You have to wade out about half a mile to get to some decent snorkelling water."

"Greece?"

"Too busy… I know - how about we go skiing? I've not been for a while and it would be good to brush the cobwebs from my skis."

Over the years, Sara has become a fair-to-middling skier. Sid usually sticks to the nursery slopes but now that Sara has mentioned it, he thought it would be adventurous to try one of the intermediate slopes for a change.

"Yeah. That sounds good. I'll get on the internet to find a decent place."

*

Inside, Lee in listening (not to be confused with Lee in lookout) made a mental note of the conversation and typed out a memo to Brian, the brain manager:

INTERNAL MEMO
From: Lee in listening
To: Brian/brain manager
Re: Sid's Xmas holiday

Brian,
I've just heard Sid discussing a Xmas holiday with Sara. They have decided to go skiing, once more. Is this anything that we need to discuss?

Lee.

Another memo with a hidden meaning…

Lee is still not fooling anyone inside, but she and Brian have agreed to at least *try* to keep their relationship a secret for the time being, even though every one of the insiders knows about it

INTERNAL MEMO

From: Brian/Brain manager
To: Lee in listening

Re: Sid's 2025 Xmas holiday

Yes, a good idea. There will be lots to discuss.
I need to inspect the Cochlea Labyrinth so I'll
meet you there.

Brian.

Handing over the controls to their respective 2IC's they both made their way down to the Cochlea Labyrinth for their 'discussion'.

Sid spent a couple of days searching the internet until he found a decent skiing venue and hotel.

*

2nd of January, 2025. Two day to go before the skiing holiday.

Back in September Sid had managed to find a cancelled booking at the ski lodge that Sara prefers, so a twelve-day holiday was booked by him. He had asked Suzy to house-sit while he and Sara were away, but Suzy told him that she would be staying at Stan's parents' home during the Christmas break. She did, however, promise to look in on the place occasionally.

Inside, there was a flurry of activity by the tiny people, all making last minute arrangements for the holiday.

Brian issued a reminder to everyone:

INTERNAL MEMO

To: All staff
From: Brian/brain manager

Re: Sid's upcoming holiday

With just 2 days to go before Sid & Sara fly off on their holiday, I remind all departments that final holiday checks should now be carried out.
All departments are to ensure that nothing is left outstanding when Sid starts his holiday. If anyone needs help with anything please let me know and I'll arrange for somebody to contact you.
Merv - It seems that you will be the busiest. Please clear down all current ideas from Sid's ideas chip and compile a new 'To Do' list for him. Your list should include the following reminders:

- *Liaise with Sara about emptying the fridge. No food is to be left to go rotten inside the fridge. Lee - please carry out a final scan of the fridge to make sure all food has been removed.*
- *Check the passports, flight details, Insurance and currency.*
- *Check the oil and water levels in the car for the journey to the airport.*

- *Confirm the airport parking arrangements.*
- *On-line Check-in at the airport.*
- *Confirm the hotel arrangements.*
- *Let the neighbours know that the house will be empty. They should have Suzy's contact details for emergencies.*
- *Let Suzy know your holiday contact details.*
- *IMPORTANT! - Remember to pack the anti-Tangier trots pills.*
- *Liaise with Lee in lookout to agree what clothes to pack and remind Sid accordingly.*
- *Lee - Please make sure that Sid homes in on just the essentials when he packs his suitcase. He always seems to take far more clothes than he needs - a complete waste of space.*

And finally - Merv, remind Sid to make sure that the house is locked down and secure on his way out.

Have a pleasant holiday everyone. Let's all give Sid a time to remember.

Brian.

*

Outside, two days later.

Every item in Sid's memory chip was addressed - almost - and he and Sara had a pleasant flight to Venice, followed by a two hour coach journey to the Barisetti Sport Hotel, Cortina d'Ampezzo, Italy.

Standing on his room's first floor balcony, taking photos of the glorious view, Sid heard Sara call his name while she unpacked the suitcases.

"Sid? Have you unpacked any of your clothes since we arrived?"

"No. Why?"

"I can't find any socks. Are you sure you packed them?"

After a moment's thought while he returned to the room, Sid replied "Yes."

"You can't have done. There are none inside either of the cases."

"I definitely got them out. I put them on the edge of the bed, next to the case."

They both looked at each other in puzzlement. Then Sara broke the silence.

"You know what? I bet you they fell off the bed while you were packing. Did you check the floor?"

"Why would I do that? I'm packing a suitcase not looking for coins that have fallen out of my pocket."

"Talking of money, you did put all the Euros in the travel bag, didn't you?"

"Er… I split the money into two, put a wedge in my wallet and then left the rest on the table for you to put in your purse."

"I didn't know that. You never said…"

Sid was now feeling a little jaded. He had no change of socks and they had only half the amount of cash they envisaged they would need for meals out, drinks, tips, presents and ski-lift fees. He would have to go into the village in the hopes that there is a hole-in-the-wall to draw out some more cash, and also find a sock shop to get some socks.

He doesn't know it yet, but his credit card is going to take a bigger hit than he presently anticipates…

160

Chapter 27
(Be prepared)

Sitting in the bar of the hotel, Sid and Sara made friends with another couple, Sergio and Sage, who had been at the resort for about five days.

"The ski lift is hellishly expensive," mentioned Sergio.

"Yeah, we've been here before, so we know about the rip-offs," answered Sid.

"Oh? Experienced skiers, then?"

"Not really. Sara is good, but I usually stick to the nursery."

"Nursery? That's for the children," a humiliating chuckle escaping from Sergio's and Sage's lips.

"Yeah, that's me. A big kid," Sid trying to make light of the conversation.

"You know what? I know of a fantastic run. It's a bit off-piste but I'm sure you'll have a great time on it," suggested Sergio.

Sara joined in. "I think we'll have fun doing what we usually do but thanks, anyway, Sergio."

Then Sage joined in. "I've seen the run that Sergio is talking about. It's a safe one, and it's got pristine snow - just right for a smooth downhill chase. I was going to do some shopping in town tomorrow, Sara, and if you join me we could spend some of our husbands' credit cards while they go and play."

Sara - "what do you think, Sid?"

Sid - "Mmm... I was thinking of giving the intermediate slope a try, but Sergio's slope? I'm not too sure."

There was a pause while Sid chewed it over.

"Okay," continued Sergio, "if you're concerned about it, Sid, you stick to the baby slopes," a supercilious look on his face. "I'm going to it tomorrow, anyway. I'll be in the lobby at about eight-fifteen if you're interested. If not, I'll go on my own."

"Where is this ski slope? Is it on Google Maps?" asked Sid, handing his phone to Sergio.

"Sure," answered Sergio typing in the co-ordinates of the off-piste ski run.

Sid briefly looked at a picture of the slope on Google Maps, then replaced the phone in his back pocket.

That night, while Sid and Sara were getting ready for bed they discussed the following day's itinerary.

"Are you going with Sergio?"

"Don't know. Not made my mind up, yet. I'm still thinking about the intermediate slope. Are you going shopping with Sage?"

"Probably, so you could be on your own for a while. I can get you some more socks while I'm in town."

"Have fun. I'll see you later," Sid replied.

*

Inside, Lee in listening (not to be confused with Lee in lookout) got on the phone to Brian, the brain manager, immediately she picked up on Sara's conversation with Sid.

"Brian, d'you remember me mentioning to you earlier that some bloke called Sergio was trying to persuade Sid to go off-piste?"

"Yeah."

"Well, I've just heard Sid discussing tomorrow's itinerary with Sara. I don't think that he has made his mind up, yet, but it seems that he's thinking about trying the intermediate slope. Is there any way Merv can send a reminder to Sid's ideas chip to reinforce the fact that going off-piste is not a wise thing to do?"

"Will do, but doesn't Sara usually do the sensible thing?"

"Yes, *usually*, but there's a strong possibility that she might go shopping with Sergios' wife, Sage."

There was a pause while Brian thought about Lee's comments.

"Do you think Sid's going off alone with this guy, Sergio?"

"I doubt it, but Sara sounds worried about it."

Another pause for thought.

"Well, we can't stop Sid from doing his own thing. We can only plant ideas for him to decide what's best for himself. I'll send out some proactive instructions, just in case Sid gets himself into some trouble. That's the best I can do at this stage."

"Thank you," answered Lee with a relieved sigh.

Brian typed out a memo.

IMPORTANT INTERNAL MEMO

To: All departments
From Brian/brain manager
This message was sent with high importance!

Re: Sid's itinerary for tomorrow.

I've just heard that Sid is probably on his way to the intermediate slope tomorrow. I've also heard from Lee in lookout that the TV has warned of heavy snowfall in the area.

Obviously, the cold is high on our list of priorities, so Merv - send a list of important items to Sid's memory chip to include in his backpack:

- *Spare socks, gloves, quilted vest and Woolly hat.*
- *Some bars of nourishment.*
- *His telephone.*
- *It might also be as well to send a negative response to going off-piste to Sid's ideas chip.*

Everyone else - ensure that your department is prepared for an unusually cold period by boosting your supply of muscle shivers to help keep Sid warm. Nick in nourishment - liaise with Fay in filters and Kevin in the kitchen to prepare for a required surge in nourishment.

Any problems - contact me immediately.

Brian.

*

Outside, after an early breakfast Sid thought to himself - for no apparent reason - *'better pack some more stuff, today.'*

Sara noticed him taking some pants and a quilted vest out of the drawer.

"Why are you packing all that stuff for the intermediate slope?" she asked.

"No specific reason. You never know when you're going to need it, do you?"

Sara shrugged, and after pecking Sid on the cheek she went down to the lobby. She had decided that a shopping trip with Sage would be fun and she left Sid filling his backpack.

She was pleased that Sid appeared to have decided against going off-piste with Sergio, and she was content that Sid was going to be okay on the intermediate slope alone. There were always plenty of people there to keep an eye on things, especially parents teaching their offsprings to ski.

Sage appeared in the lobby and the two departed from the building to find a taxi.

A few minutes later Sid checked the time on his watch and then took the lift down to the lobby with his skiing gear. Stepping through the lift doors he met Sergio exiting from an adjacent lift.

"Hi, Sid. All ready, then?"

"Yep. Let's go. I've just got to drop something into reception on my way out."

Sid had, in fact, misled Sara into thinking that he was going to the intermediate slope, and not the off-piste run with Sergio. He never lies to Sara, but when she pushed him for an answer the night before he didn't actually say that he was definitely going to the intermediate slope; but then, neither did he say that he wasn't.

The two men also departed from the building to find a taxi.

Chapter 28
(Oh, No!)

Sid and Sara are due to fly home in four days time.

They had enjoyed this trip, so far. Lots of nursery slope skiing for Sid, lots of extremely tasty Michelin starred food, lots of booze and lots of sleep. With just three days of holiday left, Sid was looking forward to returning to the UK.

Today, he was on his way to an off-piste slope with a chap called Sergio who he had met in the hotel bar.

"Are you sure this ski run is okay?" asked Sid.

"Absolutely. I've been going all week and not had any problems with it yet."

There was something at the back of Sid's mind that told him it was not wise to go off-piste, but if Sergio has been skiing there all week it must be okay… mustn't it?

The taxi dropped the men at the side of the road, in the middle of no-where. After retrieving their ski kit from the roof of the car, Sid looked round.

"It's a gorgeous view, isn't it?" asked Sergio.

"Too true. I could look at this view all day and still want more."

"Yeah, but we've got a bit of a hike to the ski run, so we'd better get a move on before we run out of time."

The two men trudged up the hillside and into the unknown.

Sara and Sage returned from their spending spree, heavily laden with shopping bags full of designer clothes and presents.

After collecting the room key from reception she went upstairs, unlocked the door and entered an empty room. She and Sage had had lunch in town, so they arrived back at the hotel mid-afternoon. It was too late to get changed and go skiing, so she decided to give Sid a call and see how he was doing on what she thought was the intermediate slope.

Sara's call went straight to voicemail.

'Oh, well,' she thought. *'he's turned his phone off.'*

She busied herself throughout the afternoon, trying on and admiring new clothes and writing emails. At about five-thirty she looked outside and saw it was getting dark.

'It'll soon be too dark to ski safely, so he'll be back soon,' she pondered. *'Anyway, the ski slopes close down at six, so he'll have to come back then.'*

Sid and Sergio had had a good time on the off-piste run.

Sergio had tutored Sid to a reasonable standard and they both ascended the hillside higher than the last run. At each new level the snow was pristine, like a pure white tablecloth spread out before them.

"You've done well this afternoon, Sid. There's no way you can restrict yourself to the baby slopes after this."

"Yeah. I do feel that I'm a better skier, thanks to your expert tutoring."

"It was nothing, and anyway, you're a quick learner. Another run?"

"It's getting dark, Sergio. We really should be making our way back. What time did you ask the taxi to pick us up?"

"Somewhere around six," looking at his watch. "There's time for one more run, then we can head back to the pick-up point."

"Okay."

Sid was game for another run. He'd had such a good time he really didn't want to leave now. For the last time today, the two men heaved themselves up the slope to a new set-off point about two hundred yards higher than the last time.

You know, virgin snow is funny stuff. Light, fluffy and full of air... and highly mobile.

The reason that all ski resorts encourage their clients to stay on the recommended ski runs is that off-piste runs are fraught with danger, particularly avalanches.

Powder snow avalanches usually occur with fresh snow that settles like dry powder. The very type that Sid and Sergio are skiing on. The avalanche is triggered by collapse of an underlying weak snow layer. Once released, it accelerates rapidly and grows in mass and volume, capturing more snow on its way down the mountainside. This type of avalanche can exceed speeds of 300 km/h (190 mph), with masses of up to 1,000,000,000 tons.

It goes without saying this, but if you are skiing in front of *any* avalanche, you need to get out of its way... Quickly!

"Look at that view," said Sid when they reached their set-off point.

"Yeah. Fantastic!" replied Sergio. "Ready?"

"Go for it."

The two men started to weave their way downhill, skiing left, then right, then left again. Their criss-cross skiing suddenly caused the underlying weak snow layer to collapse.

Sid heard the rumbling first. He was about twenty yards behind Sergio.

"SERGIO!" he shouted, to attract Sergio's attention.

Looking backwards, Sergio frantically started to drive his ski poles into the snow, at the same time shouting to Sid, "FASTER! SKI FASTER!"

Sid followed suit, occasionally looking behind himself. The avalanche was gaining on the two men and the rumbling got louder.

Pumping their arms faster and faster, the two men made a beeline for a rocky outcrop about three hundred metres to their left. It was Sergio's plan that if they could get to the outcrop before the avalanche they might stand a chance of sheltering behind a boulder.

Sid took another look behind.

"Oh, Crap!" he said out loud. The avalanche was now a mere fifty yards away and bearing down on the men rapidly. The wall of snow towered a good fifty metres above them.

Sid was unable to reach the rocky outcrop. The avalanche smothered him, picked him up and threw him around as if he was a rag doll. He felt a bump as he collided with a boulder. Then another as he was slammed into a tree. He felt himself being rolled head over heals, bouncing off the ground, then off another tree as he was thrown around by the avalanche.

Then everything went dark, and quiet, as he slipped into unconsciousness.

The moment Sid became unconscious he must have been the luckiest man alive. It seemed to be an eternity that Sid looked into the blackness, but he was unconscious for a short time only. Opening his eyes he saw clouds, and sky and the twinkling of a lone star. Good fortune had rolled him on his back and deposited his broken body at the top of the packed snow that had once been the avalanche. His head, uncovered and exposed to the elements, was the only part of his body not packed into the snow… Packed being the operative word.

He knew that his right leg was tucked under his body, but he couldn't feel his left leg. His arms were pressed into his sides, as if he had been bound and tied with coils of rope. He was unable to move.

Mustering as much force as his restricted chest would allow he shouted, "SERGIO! SERGIO, ARE YOU THERE?"

No answer.

"SERGIO!"

Again, no answer.

"HELP!"

Silence.

"ANYBODY! HELP!"

More silence.

The darkness of night began to descend. Sid was glad that he had bothered to wear all those extra clothes that he had extracted from the hotel room drawer… Except an extra pair of socks 'cos he didn't have any.

He braced himself for a long night to come…

Chapter 29
(Situation critical)

"WHAT THE BLOODY HELL HAPPENED JUST THEN?" bellowed Brian, the brain manager.

The insiders had just experienced another unexpected chaotic upheaval. A worst one than the drunken brawl at Scott and Symone's wedding. This time, furniture just didn't get upturned. Table legs were broken, equipment was smashed, an electrical fire had broken out in the server room and lots of tiny people were well and truly battered.

"Someone get that woman to the infirmary, and get me a telephone that works," continued Brian. "You there! Get me a situation report."

Merv, the message wires manager, came forward holding his elbow, the hand on his damaged arm tucked under his chin. "Sid was off-line for a few minutes. Whatever it was, that caused all this, must have been pretty dynamic."

"Yes, I figured that, Merv. Get yourself to the infirmary. I can't see Sid requiring any ideas yet. Let me know how you get on," instructed Brian.

He turned to the first tiny person that he saw was uninjured. "Go down to the lookout post and see if Lee needs any help. I need to know what Sid can see, urgently - and use the stairs. I don't know what state the lift is in."

"Yes, sir," returned the tiny person, who immediately trotted off towards the stairs.

A telephone was put in front of Brian and he dialled the number for Lee in listening. No response, just the tone that told him that Lee's number was unobtainable.

He then tried Piers, the pump manager. Same tone.

Next was Bella, the bellows manager.

Bella answered. "Bella in bellows…"

"Hi Bella, it's Brian. How you doing down there?"

"The bellows are still on-line and functioning, just, but Sid's chest is restricted in its movements so he's taking small, but frequent, breaths."

"Okay. Keep me informed, and let me know if you need anything."

"Will do. How's Lee, in listening?"

"Don't know, yet. Her phone line is down."

"Do you want me to go upstairs and see if she's okay?"

"No, you've got better things to do, Bella, but thanks anyway."

As soon as Brian put the phone down the tiny person who went off to get a situation report appeared and thrust a sheet of paper at Brian.

"Good man. Thanks," he said, taking hold of the paper.

He read the situation report, provided by the department managers:

Pump - Functioning. Regular, but requiring nourishment.
Bellow - Functioning, but restricted. Situation critical.
Lookout Post - Functioning, but sight-line is restricted. Can only focus straight ahead with limited vision sideways. It appears that Sid has been caught up in an avalanche!
Listening Post - Unknown.
Filters - Functioning. Temperature reducing, but presently tolerable.
Metabolism - Functioning, but presently tolerable.
Message wires - Unknown.
Mechanics - Unknown. Possibly some damage to his supporting stanchions and his lifters. A more detailed report will follow when a better inspection has been made. Movement - Unable to move in any direction.

Kitchen - Inoperative. One hour to bring the kitchen back on-line.

Connor, Brian's runner, had done well to get round most of the important departments. There was just the listening post and nerve section to respond, although Brian knew that Merv, the message wires manager, had reported sick. He worried about Lee in listening. The runner had been unable to access the listening post. He issued another instruction to Connor who had stood waiting for orders.

"Get back down to the listening post and see if you can get inside. Do whatever it takes. I need to know how Lee is."

"Yes, sir," and off dashed the runner.

*

Outside, Sara looked through the balcony doorway. The time was now six-fifteen, and the darkness of the night was quicky descending on the town. She telephoned down to reception.

"Good evening, Mrs. Smethers. What can I do for you?"

"Do you know if my husband has returned from the ski slope?"

There was a slight pause while the receptionist turned to look at the key press.

"It doesn't look like it, madam. His door key is still on its hook. The ski slope closed about half an hour ago."

"Thank you," responded Sara and she returned the telephone handset back to its cradle.

'Maybe he's down at the bar?' thought Sara, still not realising that Sid had decided to go off-piste.

With dinner time forty-five minutes away, Sara decided to wait for a while to see if Sid would dash into the hotel room, eager to get changed for dinner. The room telephone chirped its annoying happy little chirp. It was Sage phoning her room.

"Sara, I don't suppose you've seen Sergio, have you?"

Sara responded with just three words, "Meet me downstairs," and replaced the handset.

Sage was sat on a sofa in the reception area when Sara exited the lift.

"Did Sergio go off-piste this morning?" Sara asked.

"I think so, why?"

"Did he take Sid with him?"

"I don't know. You and I left the hotel before either of them. Did Sid say he was going with Sergio?"

"I thought he was going to the intermediate slope, but that closed at five forty-five so it's unlikely that he will still be skiing."

The two women stared at each other for a few seconds, then Sara went to the reception desk. Collaring a vacant receptionist, she asked, "Has my husband left any messages for me?"

The receptionist looked in the mail slot, looked on her PC screen and then disappeared into the back room.

Returning in about ten seconds, the receptionist advised, "No madam, there are no messages for you."

Sage had joined Sara at the reception desk. She asked the same question about Sergio. Repeating her previous search the receptionist, again, answered in the negative.

Sara glanced outside through the hotel entrance doors. It was now as dark as it was likely to get before daybreak.

She turned and declared to the receptionist, "I think our husbands are missing…"

Chapter 30
(It's going to be a long night)

The night was long and hard for Sid.

He slept little, he was cold and he hurt. To him, it felt as if he had been hit by a bus and then dragged for a hundred yards before being pulled feet first through a mangler. Of concern was his right leg that was now throbbing madly, complaining about the unusual position it had been forced to endure. He still couldn't feel his left leg, and his left arm was constantly reminding Sid what pins-and-needles really feels like.

Somehow he had to let everyone know where he was and what state he was in. He remembered his telephone. Sid thought that it may have dropped out of his back pocket when the avalanche grabbed him, but with luck it was still in there. He managed to wriggle his right hand round to his pocket and pull out the phone with his finger and thumb.

'Does it still work?' he thought.

Just by feel, he turned the phone on. He waited for a few minutes to give his arm a rest. Just as he was about to dial he felt the phone vibrate. An incoming call, but he knew that it was impossible to answer it. From the ring tone he knew it was a voicemail message but he could barely hear what the message was.

Waiting until the message had ended he searched the keypad with his finger and dialled the 113 emergency number. He knew it would be a forlorn hope to answer the operator but if he left his phone on, the authorities should be able to triangulate his position. They would surely know there was a problem if he didn't answer them, but Sid tried to alert the operator by shouting "HELP! HELP!" He had absolutely no idea if they could hear him.

Last night, when Sara told the receptionist that she thought her husband was missing, the receptionist hurried into the back room to fetch the hotel manager.

"What makes you think your husband is missing?" asked Salvatore, the manager.

"The ski slopes are closed for the night and I suspect he has gone off-piste with Sage's husband," pointing to Sage.

"And you think that *your* husband is also missing?" he asked Sage.

"Yes. He usually telephones me to let me know when he will be back, but I've not heard from him since this morning."

Looking at both women, and reaching for a sheet of paper to make notes on, he asked, "When was the last time you saw them?"

The two women looked at each other and Sara answered. "We left the hotel at about eight a.m. to go and do some shopping. We returned at mid-afternoon."

"I see. And you have still not heard from either of your husbands?"

"No." Tears formed in Sage's eyes.

Sara looked outside at the blackness of the night.

Salvatore turned to his receptionist. "Have any of the two men contacted you at all, Sabine?"

"No, sir…" She suddenly held up a finger and continued, "Wait a minute…" She turned to her PC console and typed in a few commands. Looking at the screen she confirmed, "Signor Smethers left a message with reception on his way out this morning. He told me that he was going with Signor Sergio and he left his mobile number in case anyone needed to contact him."

Salvatore looked at the screen and wrote Sid's phone number on his sheet of paper. He picked up the telephone receiver, dialled the number and waited. The call went straight to Sid's voicemail.

"He's not answering," advised Salvatore.

He once more turned to his receptionist. "Phone the avalanche management control centre and ask if they have been active today."

While the party waited for an answer, Sergio's taxi driver entered the hotel and made a beeline for the reception desk.

"Can you please see if Signor Smethers and his friend have returned to the hotel? I was supposed to pick them up earlier, but they never turned up at the pick-up point."

A silence descended on the group surrounding the end of the reception desk. The taxi driver looked at each one, in turn.

The receptionist looked up and said to Salvatore, "The avalanche control centre confirms that they have not been active, but there is a report of a hard slab avalanche close to the Località Cadin di Sotto."

The taxi driver spoke up. "That's where I dropped the two men this morning."

Another pregnant pause while this comment sank in.

Salvatore then picked up the telephone and dialled the 113 emergency number.

There was a lengthy conversation, and the manager returned the phone handset to its cradle.

"Someone from the search and rescue authority is on his way here. Please take a seat in the lounge and I will bring a tray of coffee out to you."

The two women and the taxi driver turned and went to a circle of chairs in the lounge.

After about half an hour Severo, the search and rescue chap, entered the hotel and was pointed towards the women. Sage was crying into her hankie.

"Good evening, ladies. I understand that you think your husbands are missing."

Sara's patience was now beginning to slip.

"I don't think... I *know* they are both in some sort of trouble. It's now eight-thirty and it's been twelve and a half hours since either of us saw them and I am deeply concerned about my husband's welfare."

"I understand that, Mrs. Smethers, but there is little we can do until first light tomorrow. It is too dangerous for any of my team to go out looking for them if, as I am told, there is a propensity of avalanches in the area you think your husbands have been skiing. We must hope that they have found some safe haven somewhere until the morning but I promise you, we will be out at the crack of dawn to search for them."

"What about a helicopter. Don't they have infra-red search lights?"

"It is far too dangerous to send out a helicopter in the darkness. That area is surrounded by mountains. The helicopter could fly into one without realising it. No, we have to be patient. If your husband doesn't return before morning I will send every available person out to look for him. I have to say, however, that *if*, and we don't know *anything* yet, but *if* he has been caught up in an avalanche then you must be prepared for the worst..."

Sage sobbed out loud.

With nothing more to be said, or done, everyone went to their beds. It was doubtful, however, that either of the women would sleep. For them, and their husbands, it was going to be a long night.

Chapter 31
(Brrr! It's freezing)

Inside, Brian became increasingly concerned about the state of Sid's physiology.

Sid's extremities were, according to Tommy, the temperature manager, getting colder, something that usually happens, Brian recalls, when Sid's hands and feet are losing heat faster than heat can be produced by his body. Merv had activated one of Sid's ideas chips to try to persuade him that more physical exercise is useful in creating body heat and Tommy had cranked up Sid's shiver activity to keep his muscles warm.

Nothing seemed to be working, so Brian assumed that there was a big problem outside.

Despite any problems that the outsiders might be experiencing, he had problems of his own, not least his inability to communicate with the departments. His thoughts were to concentrate on the inside problems and let the outsiders concentrate on theirs. With luck, he will be able to keep Sid alive until the outside problems had been un-problemed.

Picking his phone up, he contacted his runner. "Connor, have you managed to secure access to the listening department, yet?"

"Yes, sir. I have Lee, the listening manager next to me. I'll pass you over."

With a sigh of relief, Brian heard Lee's voice. "Hello, you. How are things upstairs? It's been pretty chaotic down here, but I've managed to get a team together and Sid's hearing is now one hundred percent."

"Am I glad to hear your voice… I was a bit worried, there, for a moment. Are you injured in any way?"

"Nothing serious, lover. Just a few minor cuts and bruises. Nothing to stop us meeting."

"Glad to hear that, Lee. I don't know what I'd do without you. How's your team. It's no good me asking if you need any help because I don't have anyone."

"No problem, Brian. Everyone is okay. I'll return your runner to you. See you later."

The call was terminated and Brian typed out a message to be distributed when his runner had returned to him. The message would have to be sent round by hand because the computer server room was not yet fully up and running, although the fire had, by now, been extinguished.

INTERNAL MEMO

To: All departments
From: Brian/brain manager

Re: Sid's status

My runner has returned with your short reports. Thank you, all. Can you now please provide a detailed report on Sid's status, asap?
I think that we now have the reason why chaos descended upon us recently. I am advised by Lee in lookout that he may well have been caught up in an avalanche while he was skiing.
Tommy - I am concerned about Sid's decreasing temperature. I know you are working hard to increase his body heat, but if there is anything else that you can do to fend off the cold I'm sure Sid will appreciate it. Also, inform me the minute Sid's temperature drops below 35°C.

Bella - I know it is difficult, but somehow try to increase Sid's intake of oxygen. All departments need as much as the bellows can send to them.

Merv - Somehow get a message to Sid's chips to make him stay awake. If necessary take it to the chips and install it manually using the backup server. I need him to be awake if ... when help arrives to dig him out of the snow.

Everyone - Sid is close to suffering from Hypothermia. His normal body temperature of 37°C is dropping. If there is anything that can be done to delay the onset of frostbite and later gangrene you must take those steps now, before Sid suffers catastrophic damage.

Please keep me informed of any changes in Sid's status via a runner from your department until all communications are returned to normal.

IT IS ESSENTIAL THAT YOU ALL KEEP WARM!

Brian.

The tiny people inside Sid were all now wearing their overcoats and scarves and hats and gloves and thick woolly socks to fend off the cold atmosphere that was descending on their departments.

Their breath condensed on the cold walls and ice was beginning to form on the exposed surfaces. With little else to do - the systems were still off-line - they ran on the spot and jumped up and down to try to keep warm. Small groups of tiny people were gathered together by the department managers for some PT, and those on standby, the reserve force, all brought their sheets and blankets to their respective department to pass around the tiny people.

Kevin, in the kitchen, instructed his staff to generate more nourishment and force this into the nourishment tubes as fast as possible. Mick, the masher, and Fred, the food shoveller joined them to help out and keep warm.

As soon as Brian's runner appeared in the doorway he was given the message to distribute to all departments. This tiny person is a really fit guy. Presently, he is the luckiest guy inside because he is kept warm by all the exercise that he is getting.

*

Outside, the sun's slow ascent over the horizon was a godsend to Sid. Shivering furiously, he welcomed the warming effect of the sun's rays on his face.

His thoughts turned back time to when Sara had mocked him for packing so much extra clothing. Without those extra pairs of underpants, and a quilted vest, and spare T-shirt he doubted that he would have lasted the night out.

It was now difficult for him to remain conscious as drowsiness cloaked him like a dark, sinister shroud, but he knew that if he succumbed to the alluring effects of his drowsiness he would surely freeze to death.

His breathing wasn't normal at the best of time, due to the crushing effects of the snow tightly packed around his chest, but he continued his fight to take slow, shallow breaths. He knew that the cold was gradually seeping into his body and sapping his strength, but he didn't give up hope that a rescue party would arrive to dig him out.

Back at the hotel, long before the sun eased itself over the horizon, Severo, the search and rescue organiser, had assembled his team, tested all the equipment, carried out the radio checks, patted the dogs' heads and he was ready to go.

Sara and Sage offered to go with the team, but were persuaded to stay at the hotel where they would be warm, dry and on hand to let Severo know if Sid and Sergio arrived back.

The search and rescue party departed in their assortment of cars, vans and trucks.

Sid knew that he had to stay awake. Occasionally, he would attempt to shout for help, but his strength was now well and truly sapped, so all he could manage was a plaintive moan.

As the sun rose higher in the sky his strength eventually gave up on him.

*

Inside Sid, the tiny people were all now lying on the floor of their departments.

Curled up in tiny balls, knees pulled up to their chests, they were in the same semi-conscious state as Sid. They lay there, waiting for the inevitable eternal sleep that they all knew was the only outcome for them.

Brian did his best to keep the tiny people awake but even he eventually laid down and surrendered to the cold.

*

Outside, Sid closed his eyes to savour the heat of the sun on his face, but he knew that that would not be enough to keep him warm. He thought he heard the sound of a helicopter, but when he looked up at the sky he saw

185

nothing. It must have been an audible mirage. Closing his eyes again he pictured Sara.

It was now well over twenty four hours since the avalanche had eaten Sid, chewed him up and partially spat him out.

With his eyes closed, he started to give up on being found and his thoughts were diverted away from Sara to what people would think of his strange attire when he finally emerged from the ice in the spring thaw.

He had stopped shivering and he could no longer feel the pain of his body. His hands and feet were numb and he had lost all feeling in his right leg. He knew that time was running out for him. He sensed that the darkness of death was close by, waiting to embrace him in an eternal sleep.

His mind's eye was brought back to his vision of Sara. He remembered how lovely she looked on their wedding day and he felt sad that he was not able to say goodbye to her. He wondered if this was the last vision of her that he would see. He wondered how she would cope without him. He wondered how long she would grieve, and if she would meet someone else? Would she share her bed, again, but with someone else?

His vibrant vision of Sara smiled at him and kissed his lips, his eyes and his forehead, over and over again. He felt her breath on his cheeks. In his near unconscious state he thought to himself, *'Blimey, Sara. Your breath smells!'*

WHAT? Why did he think that? Sara's breath isn't all that bad!

Mustering as much will power as he could raise, he half opened his eyes to see the blurred image of a dog's wet nose and lapping tongue licking every inch of his exposed face. He then heard the shouts of the search and rescue party, their boots crunching through the snow.

An oxygen mask was roughly pushed onto his nose and mouth and he heard the sound of hands scraping the snow away from his head and shoulders. He felt lots of hands stripping his clothes from him to instal the suction pads of a heart monitor to his chest, and he heard the rescue team shouting "Stay with us! Stay with us! Open your eyes," not that he had the strength to keep his eyelids open.

All he wanted to do was go to sleep...

Chapter 32
(Ouch!)

When Sid eventually opened his eyes the first thing he saw were the strip lights of a private hospital room.

Hearing the heart machine, with its monotonous regular beep, he turned his head to get a better understanding of his surroundings. A nurse was adjusting a dial on the machine and out of the corner of her eye she saw Sid stir.

"Ah, you're back with us," she said, with a sexy Italian lilt.

Leaning down to fluff his pillows, she smiled a beautiful white smile and helped Sid sit up. At first he was a little light headed, but that soon wore off and he felt like talking.

"What time is it? How long have I been here?"

"Oh… They found over twenty four hours ago. We've had to keep you sleeping all this time so as to stabilise your condition, but once you were able to cope we took you off those meds. It's almost seven p.m."

Sid let the information sink in for a few moments while he took stock of his condition. His right leg was in traction and his left arm was encased in a plaster. Right now he decided against trying to move those limbs, but his other arm and leg didn't appear to have suffered so much. He looked at his heavily bandaged hands.

"What's wrong with these?" he asked the nurse.

"You were extremely lucky," she replied. "We almost had to amputate some fingers, but once the frostbite had been removed it seems that they will heal okay. Your toes are the same."

Sid tried to wriggle his toes but it was too painful. His hands were the same.

"… And the traction?"

"Well, your wrist was fractured so we had to sort out a few of the bones and put them back where they belonged. You may have noticed the pins sticking out of the end of your fingers. Be careful not to catch those on anything because they will hurt for a while. Your leg had what's called a compound fracture of the Femur. We've had to put a plate and some screws in that to support the fracture while it heals. You've got more pins, plates and screws than my car, and you have a few broken ribs but they will heal on their own."

"How long am I going to be tied up, like this?" pointing to the traction equipment.

"You won't be going anywhere soon. We're looking at a minimum of two months before the traction is taken off. Then there is probably another two to three months of convalescence."

"What date is it?"

"It's the tenth"

Sid digested the answer. He remembered that he spent the night on the mountainside, trapped in the snow. That would be the night of the eighth/ninth. The nurse told him he had been out of it for twenty four hours, so if today is the tenth, tomorrow is the eleventh.

"I'm supposed to fly home tomorrow," he said.

"That's not going to happen, is it? Your wife is here. I'll send her in?"

"Yes, please"

The nurse fussed around Sid's bed for a while, tidying his bedclothes and checking the various machines that he was plugged into, and she then left the room to find Sara.

The first words that came from Sara's mouth were "You idiot!"

"It's lovely to see you, too, Sara."

"What were you thinking, going off-piste?" she reprimanded. "You know how dangerous it is. You've always known how dangerous it is. We talked about this every time we go skiing, Sid, and you know that the golden rule is to stay away from unregistered slopes." Tears began to well up in her eyes.

"I'm truly sorry, Sara. You don't think I wanted to end up like this, do you?"

"Of course not, but you should have known better, you stupid idiot."

With his good arm he hugged Sara as best he could, groaning about the pain from his rib cage in the process.

"True, every word," he admitted. "How did they find me?"

Dabbing the tears from her eyes, Sara answered, "You left the co-ordinates at reception, but that wouldn't have helped much because they didn't know there was an avalanche in that area until we asked. The receptionist you left the information with had gone off duty by the time we realised you were missing, and the new receptionist hadn't even opened the reception PC to pick up any messages.

"Anyway, they managed to get your location by pinging your phone. A helicopter flew over the area and saw your idiot face poking out of the snow. You've no idea just how lucky you are, Sid."

It would take Sara a long time to forgive Sid, if she ever did.

He told her about the conversation he had had with the nurse, particularly with regard to the time scale involved with this hospital trip.

"I've notified the insurers," advised Sara, "and they're sending a man to interview the surgeon. They have, however, authorised your treatment here because it is cheaper than flying you home in an air ambulance. It seems that our insurers know and trust this particular hospital to get on with things without charging the earth."

"That's one good thing - money well spent on that policy," came back Sid. Sara just gave him an icy stare.

Sid suddenly remembered his partner in crime.

"How's Sergio?" he asked.

"They never found him. They won't find him until the spring thaw. They spent many hours searching for him, but even the search dog was unable to sniff him out. Sage took the first available flight home when the search for him was called off."

Sid sighed and bowed his head in sadness... He now realised just how lucky he had been.

*

Inside, the really tiny people were thankful that he had been rescued. Any longer, with the cold slowly percolating into every internal department and system, and they would surely have all died. Fortunately, the dog with the bad breath had found Sid in time.

As soon as Sid was prised from his tomb of snow and wrapped in a shiny blanket his body temperature slowly stabilised and began to rise. This was helped along by the warmth provided by the search helicopter's ambient temperature.

Merv, the message manager got a "Well done!" from Brian for planting the suggestion to take extra clothing into Sid's ideas chip. The extra layers certainly helped to fend off the cold for a longer period than if he had been wearing just his normal skiing gear.

It turns out that the runner was the only tiny person to have survived intact. Everyone else had laid on the floor and succumbed to the cold by falling asleep. The runner's regime of running everywhere had kept him relatively warm and consequently kept the cold at bay.

At the time it felt like he was the only person on earth and he wandered around for a while in a lonely quest to find someone, anyone, not sleeping. Returning to the brain department he tried to stir a couple of the tiny people, but he eventually adopted the 'Buddy' system of keeping Brian and himself warm by embracing Brian and covering them both with a spare blanket.

Brian slowly recovered and immediately he was back on his feet he thanked the runner for his timely action. The runner informed him that he, the runner, had tried to cover as many of the tiny folk that he could.

Until Sid was found by the dog with the bad breath, Brian covered himself with as many spare blankets that he could find and busied himself re-booting the undamaged servers back to life. He went round the brain department returning desks and PC's to their proper places and then performed tests on the PC's to find the ones that worked. His time was well spent getting Sid's internal systems back on-line. He despatched the runner to do what he can to help anyone that showed any signs of recovery.

By the time Sid stirred from his slumber in the hospital bed, all the tiny people in all the departments had warmed up and had awakened from their own uninvited slumbers. Hours were spent in the clean-up operation. The ice-covered surfaces in every department - the ceilings, walls, floors, furniture, equipment and, indeed the people - had slowly thawed and water sloshed around on the floor.

This had to be cleared up and everywhere thoroughly dried off before anyone was allowed anywhere near an electrical outlet. Furniture had to be replaced and equipment had to be tested. Fortunately most of the servers had suffered just minor damage and, once dried off, were serviceable.

Thanks to Brian's work while the tiny people slept, the PC screens lit up with the welcome page and most people were able to work on Sid's systems, once more.

Brian summoned Max, Bella, Piers, Billy, Nick, Kevin and Tommy to the brain department for an emergency ZEBRA (Zone Emergency Briefing Room A) meeting.

"Settle down folks. Have you all brought a pad and pens with you?"

Everyone took their seat and nodded in answer to Brian's question.

"Okay. All I want right now is a brief summary of your departments' status. Tommy…"

"Sid's temperature has returned to normal. Merv deserves a medal for suggesting that Sid should take more coverings. That certainly made a big difference to Sid when he needed to keep his temperature up."

"Yeah, already spoken to Merv. Billy…"

"Morning all. Sid's big wrapping took a big hit to his extremities. Although he has suffered frostbite, the damaged wrapping has been surgically removed by the outsiders and his extremities are now temporarily wrapped in bandages. I understand from Lee in listening that his extremities will be monitored by the outsiders and his wrappings changed regularly."

"Any other damage?"

"Well, yes. One of his supporting stanchions was snapped and one end was pushed through the wrapping and exposed to the outside. Max will be able to tell you more about the stanchion, but the outsiders have sown up his wrapping in that area and I think it will heal in due course."

"Good. I'll come to the mechanics in a moment, Max. Kevin…"

"Hello everyone. It's good to see you are all okay. Nick and I got a bit…"

Kevin was interrupted by an impatient Brian. "Get on with it, Kevin."

"Oh, right, sorry. The kitchen is back up and running and Nick's team.." showing a hand in Nick's direction, "..is busy processing some nourishment for distribution. We're about eighty-five percent up to full productivity, but we should be one hundred percent when the rest of my crew return from the sick bay. The outsiders have attached a lifter to a temporary external nourishment tube until Sid is in a state to take in solids."

"Good. You want to add anything, Nick?"

"Yes, thank you. Billy may have noticed some discoloration of the wrapping in some areas, especially around the area that was breached by a stanchion."

Billy nodded in agreement.

"This was caused by damage to his nourishment tubes, but I've repaired all the damaged tubes and the discoloration should pass soon enough."

"Well done. Bella…"

"Hello everyone. The bellows are functional, with some discomfort because Sid's bellows cage has taken a big hit. Otherwise, everyone and everything is up and running."

"Good. Max, your turn…"

"Thank you. Sid's right supporting stanchion was snapped. The protruding end of the stanchion was surgically brought back in line by the outsiders, and the two broken ends of this were paired up by the outsider's surgical team. Plates have been screwed over the broken stanchion, by them, to support this until I can weld a more permanent repair. Presently, his leg is being stretched to assist with the healing process. It'll take me a few months - outside world time - to make a permanent repair but once that's done Sid can be taken off the stretching machine and he can begin to learn to walk again."

Max turned a few pages of his notes over and continued, "The joint on his left lifter got knocked out of position and some of his grabbers were dislocated or broken. Again, the outside surgical team re-located the small components and Sid's fingers are now held in place with pins until more permanent repairs can be made. He's now got more pins, plates and screws in him than what's in my workshop. I'll keep you informed of progress."

"Excellent. Finally, Piers…"

"Sid suffered for about twenty four hours before the cold eventually took its toll and stopped the servers working. It was just by good fortune that a dog with bad breath found him and warmed his face with some licks to it. Unfortunately Sid's pump stopped working while the outsiders were digging him out of the snow. However, the cold that stopped him working effectively helped quite a lot by preserving Sid's internals until the outsiders managed to restart his pump. His pump, though, suffered from some irreparable damage and he now has a pump Arrythmia which may cause some problems in the future."

"A pump Arrythmia?" asked Bella.

"It's a pump rhythm that isn't normal. Sid will feel this as a fluttering, a racing or a pounding pump beat. Now, Arrythmias range from harmless to serious. The outcome varies, greatly, on the type of Arrythmia affecting the pump, but I can't give you any more information until I've completed a full inspection. Suffice to say that I'm a bit worried."

There was a pregnant pause as everyone digested Piers' report. Brian was the first to speak.

"Well, everyone. I think we all now have a better picture of Sid's status. Please make sure you pass on to everyone in your departments everything we've discussed this morning."

Turning to his runner, Brian continued, "Before you go, we all owe a debt of gratitude to Connor, my runner. He kept me from falling into the big sleep, and he went round covering you all up after he had revived me. I think that deserves more than a round of applause from everyone, so I'm going to promote him to Courier and Keep Fit manager."

Everyone stood and gave the runner a standing ovation. Brian then issued instructions to Connor. "Congratulations, Connor. Please type up the notes on this morning's meeting and distribute them to all departments. Thank you, all, for your time and valued comments. Fall out and return to your duties."

The ZEBRA group exited the brain department, busily chatting about the information they had all shared. Brian called Piers back before he reached the door.

"Piers. I want you to give me a daily report on Sid's pump and what is being done by the outsiders to make Sid more comfortable. Don't write a book. A couple of lines will do… And don't let the others know what you are reporting to me."

"No, sir."

Piers departed, and Brian sat in deep contemplation behind his desk trying not to think of the ramifications of Piers' report…

Chapter 33
(Sid's repairs)

It is now eighteen months since Sid's skiing incident.

Sid was released from the Italian hospital three months after he had been admitted. At the time, he hobbled around on crutches and he and Sara were eventually repatriated back to the UK by his accident insurer.

The incident had been a close call for him *and* the tiny people inside, but everyone inside all managed to repair themselves, repair their environments and repair what they could of Sid's damaged body parts. His fractured leg took several more months to heal properly, and after many visits to his local hospital he was eventually signed off.

Brian called Max up to his office.

"Good morning, Max. Lee, in lookout, tells me that Sid has been to hospital to get signed off his sick file."

"Yes, sir. I've welded the snapped stanchion together and his full weight is now distributed equally between both supporting stanchions without any supplementary supports (*aka crutches*). The plates and screws have been left attached to his supporting stanchion, and I'm slowly covering these with extra stanchion material (*aka bone calcium*). This will add strength to his stanchion, but Lee in listening told me that Sid has been advised not to do any more skiing. The strain may create further damage to his stanchion."

"Yes, Lee has told me that, as well. Can't be a bad thing," said Brian. "We can all do without another skiing incident like the last one."

"Yes, that's true, sir. Sid now really needs to get himself as fit as he was before he was taken to hospital. Is there any way you can suggest that to him?"

"Yes, of course. A good idea. A fitness regime will do us all some good, I'm sure. I'll see to it as soon as we've finished here." Brian made a note in his notebook. "What about the rest of his supporting structure?"

"Well, I've siphoned off all the excess lubricant in the joint in his lifter and the size of his joint has returned to normal. The joint has healed up to one hundred percent capacity and Sid is now using this regularly. The supporting vessel was removed several months ago. The broken bars (*aka ribs*) in his bellows cage have also been welded by me and I understand from Bella that his bellows are fully functional."

"Excellent...," there was a pause while Brian referred to his notebook, "...and his big wrapping?"

"I do know that the wrapping in the area of his snapped stanchion has healed over and all the supporting ropes (*aka stitches*) have been removed. There will always be a gash mark in that area, but I'm sure Sid will live with that. As far as any other area of wrapping is concerned you'll have to speak to Billy about that, sir."

"Okay. Well done with the work you have done to get Sid back on his feet. Fall out, and keep me informed of any problems."

"Yes, sir." Max turned and left the brain department.

Brian made a note to have a word with Billy, but Brian's attitude is 'no news is good news', so Billy's discussion will have to wait until Brian's got some spare time.

He turned to Merv. "Merv. Can you send a message to Sid's ideas chip to get some exercise. As soon as he responds, let me know and I'll prepare a fitness programme for all departments." He made another note in his book to remind him to devise a fitness programme for the tiny people.

*

200

Outside, sat at the breakfast table one morning, Sid eyed the plate of food that Sara placed in front of him.

Two sausages, two fried eggs, two hash browns, numerous button mushrooms, two slices of fried bread, two fried tomatoes, two spoons of baked beans and two roundels of black pudding, with two rounds of toast and marmalade to follow.

Two of everything except the button mushrooms. Sid never counted the mushrooms, but he could always see that there were more than two. Over the years, Sara had always given Sid a hearty breakfast, her philosophy being that it was the most important meal of the day, so Sid was always provided with a full plate.

Now, Sid always knew his breakfasts were too much, but what could he say? Sara was a good wife and a good cook, a combination that guaranteed a delicious cholesterol filled meal at any time of the day. However, he had learned from experience that if he told Sara that he wanted to have less of something, meaning not such a large portion, she never gave it to him - ever, again. On the other hand, if he told her that he enjoyed something, that would guarantee him getting it with absolutely everything he ate. So he learned to say nothing about his meals and let Sara do what she did best - feed him.

Anyway, this particular morning his gaze alternated between his plate full of breakfast and his now expanding stomach. He took the bull by the horns and decided to broach the delicate subject of meal portions.

"You know, this is a lot of food for one meal. You do realise that I'm putting on too much weight, don't you?"

"I hadn't noticed."

Sid grabbed a handful of one of his love handles. "Look," he said, "since my skiing accident I've done nothing to stop my belt getting tighter. I've had to use a couple of notches away from my usual belt notch because I've put on so much weight."

"Perhaps you should start exercising?"

"You know what? That idea struck me yesterday, and I've been thinking what I can do to make exercising more appealing. I'll pop down to the gym today and ask what the subscription is."

"Before you do that, you should start with something a bit gentler. Perhaps some casual walking. Build it up gradually."

"Yeah, maybe," answered Sid, wiping up his egg yoke with a piece of fried bread.

Now, Sid is not one to do things half-heartedly. Whatever he did, he did it with gusto, so after breakfast he drove into town to go look-see at the gymnasium facilities. Impressed with what he saw, he eagerly signed up for a twelve month subscription and returned home to hunt out his track suit and jogging shoes.

He was determined to lose some weight.

*

Inside, Brian got a call from Lee in listening (not to be confused with Lee in lookout). "Brian, this morning I heard Sid and Sara talking about Sid losing some weight, and Lee in lookout has told me that Sid has been to take out a subscription at his local gymnasium. Do you think we should meet up somewhere to discuss this?"

Brian knew there was a hidden message in Lee's question…

Chapter 34
(Let's get fit)

Monday. The first day of Sid's fitness regime.

On arrival at the gym he was shown around and sent to the changing room to get changed into his tracksuit and gym shoes. He nervously returned to the main gym area and was greeted by Shane, Sid's personal trainer.

Shane looked Sid up and down, tutted, then invited Sid to accompany him around the equipment to familiarise himself with the equipment's use. Sid was shown an assortment of bicycles, treadmills, rowing machines, shoulder, chest and abdominal presses, and the usual barbells and dumbbells that one would meet in a get fit establishment. They returned to the first bit of equipment that Sid had been shown - the treadmill.

After being advised to "..take things slowly, at first," Sid mounted the platform, started the machine and began his warm-up jog. The trainer left him to it and went to help someone else.

After about five minutes, Sid had to reduce the platform's speed to a walking pace. He was amazed at just how unfit he was!

*

Inside, Brian picked up the telephone handset chirping at him from the desktop.

"Good morning, Bella. What can I do for you?"

"Hiya, Brian. Sid's bellows have suddenly been made to increase input. Has anything happened to make the bellows work harder?"

"Wasn't immediately aware of anything, but I'll ask around and get back to you."

Brian cut the call and dialled Lee in listening (not to be confused with Lee in lookout).

"Lee? Have you heard about anything that might make Sid's bellows work harder?"

"Yes, Lee in lookout will probably have more for you, but I heard Sid being shown around some gym equipment."

"Okay, I'll speak to Lee. Are you still on for tonight?"

"You bet. I've persuaded Kevin, in the kitchen, to make up a table for us and he's going to give us a meal to remember."

"Oh? You got something special planned?"

"I'm not saying, but there is something I want to ask you."

"Okay. See you later."

Call terminated, Brian phoned Lee in lookout (not be confused with … I think you've got the idea, by now.)

"Lee, I've just spoken to Lee in listening. She tells me that you might have some info about why Sid's bellows have been made to work harder."

"Yes, I'm presently looking at a blank wall, but Sid has been shown round a load of gym equipment and I watched as he got on a moving platform belt. It seems that he has decided to get some exercise and I guess that's what's causing Sid's bellows to increase input."

"Oh, okay. That answers questions. Anything else to report?"

"No. Good luck for tonight."

Before Brian could question Lee's last comment, Lee dropped the connection. With some puzzlement Brian typed out an internal memo to all departments.

To: All departments
From: Brian/ brain department

Re: Sid's present activity

I've just heard from Lee in listening and Lee in lookout that Sid has started his fitness regime.
Be aware of any increased activity in your department's functions and inform me of any problems that Sid might have as a consequence of his increased exercise.

Brian.

A couple of minutes after the memo was sent Brian got a phone call from Piers.

"Brian, just received your memo. Have you got time to come down to my place?"

"Sure. Fifteen minutes?"

"Yep, a good time for me. See you then."

This call terminated, Brian's phone immediately chirped away, once more.

"Brian, this is Tommy in temperature. Got your memo. Sid's temperature is rising rapidly. It's not reached an uncomfortable level, yet, but it won't be long."

"Keep an eye on it, Tommy and let me know if Sid's temperature gets out of hand. Get Theola to give you a hand."

Theola is the thermoregulators (aka sweat glands) manager.

"Will do. Good luck tonight." Answered Tommy.

Now, that's twice that that comment has been made to Brian.

Brian made his way down to the pump department to meet up with Piers.

"Hi Brian. Thanks for coming down. I would have gone up to your place but I'm monitoring Sid's pump and I didn't want to leave it with my 2IC."

"No problem, Piers. What you got for me?"

"Well, I'm a bit concerned that Sid might overdo this exercise thing. He's clearly not as fit as he was before his skiing accident, but I suppose that can be expected, given the amount of time he's been recovering. Do you think it worthwhile sending a message to Sid's ideas chip to take it easy for a while?"

"Yeah, will do. What's the status on the pump?"

"It was up to one-forty about ten minutes ago, but it slowed to around one hundred and ten when he stopped running. The needle is now on one hundred."

"Right. What's his normal pump rate?"

"Between sixty and a hundred."

"Okay. Keep me informed of any changes."

"There's one other thing…" Piers hesitated. "He has a slight pump murmur. He's had this for some time now, but his skiing incident seems to have made it worse."

"Oh? Is that controllable?"

"It is, for the time being, but if he puts the pump under lots of unnecessary stress I'm going to have my work cut out stabilising it. It's anybody's guess what happens next."

"Well, do what you can…And let me know if things deteriorate."

"Of course."

Brian turned to leave the department. On his way to the doorway Piers called after him, "Have a good time tonight, and good luck."

Brian stopped in his tracks and turned back to Piers. "That's the third time someone has wished me luck. What do you guys know that I don't?"

"Ooops! Didn't know that you didn't know. Better to ask Lee when you meet her for dinner."

On his way back upstairs, Brian was deep in thought. *'How come everyone knows about my dinner date with Lee, and why the hell do they keep wishing me luck?'*

Purely by coincidence, on his way back to the brain department Brian saw Kevin's 2IC amble passed a T-junction.

"Oi! You! What's going on?"

"With what, sir?"

"With what? With my dinner tonight with Lee in listening."

There was a long pause while Kevin's 2IC thought up a suitable answer.

"Er, Kevin knows more than me, sir."

"I don't care about what Kevin knows, I'm asking you what **you** know!" A response made with some force.

"I… I… I'm not supposed to say, sir. Can't you ask Kevin?"

"Alright. I won't embarrass you any further. Get off with you."

"Thank you, sir," and the 2IC scurried off to his initial destination.

Brian made a mental note to grill Kevin (no pun intended).

On returning to his office, Brian typed out another memo to all departments.

INTERNAL MEMO

To: All departments
From: Brian/ brain department

Re: Fitness

It is incumbent on us all to stay fit and active for Sid's sake. With this in mind, I'm going to ask Lee in lookout to keep an eye on Sid's diary entries and to notify you all of the dates that Sid writes down for his gymnasium visits.
In future, when Sid goes to the gymnasium, all unessential staff will muster in the dance hall for a programme of exercise that Piers will prepare.
The only persons excused will be Max in mechanics, Bella in bellows, Tommy in temperature and Piers in the pump room. Everyone else WILL attend. Lee from listening will take the muster parade and check off all names.

Kevin. Please report to my office asap.

Brian.

There was a lot of exasperated huffing and puffing shortly after this memo was distributed. Not everyone looked forward to Brian's fitness regime…

Chapter 35
(Uh?)

That evening, Brian entered the kitchen early with the intention of collaring Kevin.

"Good evening Brian. This way, please. I've got a table ready for you and Lee, and I've prepared a meal you'll never forget."

"Before we go any further, Kevin, how come everyone inside knows about this before I do?"

"Ah, that would be my fault." Kevin looked down in embarrassment. "When Lee came to book the meal she did tell me not to say anything to anyone, but I had to mention it to my 2IC who prepared the dessert. You know what a big mouth he's got, and I presume that he's passed it round to everyone. I apologise for that. I think Lee's going to ask you something."

"I figured that, from what I've been told. Do you know what?"

"No, afraid not. She didn't let on about that at all, but it must be important."

"Okay... Look out, she's just come out of the lift."

All day, people had been wishing Brian "..Good luck.." He kept asking himself why everyone knew what the dinner with Lee was all about except himself - and Lee had told him that she wanted to ask him an important question. What was it that was so important that it required a posh dinner to ask him?

These questions rolled around inside Brian's head, repeating themselves until he decided that there was only one question this important.

Brian and Lee had been an item for some time now, at least two years (inside world time). He had often tried asking her to marry him, but he could never find the best time, and even when the time was right he always bottled out.

Maybe she had got fed up with waiting and had decided to pop the question herself... Tonight? Brian knew the answer that he would give to her. He would say a resounding "Yes." He steeled himself to face the question as Lee walked out of the lift in the direction of the two men. She gave Brian a peck on the cheek and looked at Kevin.

Kevin broke the silence. "Your table awaits you, madame," in a poor imitation of a French inflection, a napkin draped over his arm.

At the table Brian and Lee made small talk while each meal course was served. It was the most delicious four-course meal that either of them had ever tasted. Kevin and his team really pulled out all stops to give them a meal to remember, and very little was scraped into the waste chute from Brian's and Lee's plates.

As they sat, staring at each other with longing eyes, drinking wine and relaxing in the low lights of the romantic atmosphere, Brian eventually plucked up the courage to prompt Lee to ask her question. That question. The one so important that it required a candle-lit romantic dinner in the privacy of the kitchen.

As nonchalantly as possible, Brian said, "So what's this *'important'* question you wanted to ask me?"

"Oh, yes. I almost forgot..."

'Uh? She almost forgot?' thought Brian.

Lee continued, "Can you get me some new microphones? The ones I'm using have just about reached their sell-by date."

210

This hit Brian like a punch in the stomach from big Max, the mechanic. That was definitely not the question he expected.

With a hint of animosity in his voice He replied, "You've gone to all this trouble to ask me for some new microphones?"

"Uh? No. I thought it would be nice to have a lovely meal together. We don't often do this. What did you think the meal was for - payment in kind?" with more animosity than Brian.

"No, of course not." Brian's palms facing upwards in exasperation. "I didn't think anything like that. I just didn't know."

Lee stood up, threw her napkin on the table and retorted, "I don't know what you think I am, or why I arranged this meal, but it was certainly NOT to satisfy your ego… Or anything else you had in mind."

With that, she stormed out of the kitchen.

Brian sat back in his chair and watched Lee glare at him as the lift doors closed. He was absolutely stunned. Dumbfounded. Speechless. What happened there? He looked across at Kevin who shrugged his shoulders as he folded his arms across his chest.

Only one thought entered Brian's head as he stood to leave the kitchen - *'I'll never understand women, especially that one…'*

Chapter 36
(Phew! Sweaty…)

Outside on Wednesday.

Sid has decided to go down to the gym on alternate days of the week, with the weekend being his R&R period.

Returning to the gym at nine a.m., he was instructed by Shane, his personal trainer, to warm up on the treadmill. This time he regulated his speed to a more pedestrian rate until his muscles acclimatised themselves to the increased workload.

*

Inside, Max, in mechanics, phoned Brian.

"Good morning Brian. Sid has just started his exercising. All is well at the moment. He's taking things easy for the time being, so his frame is not being put under much stress. I'll keep my eyes on the stress gauges and let you know if he oversteps the mark. Has your keep fit session started yet?"

"Yep. Everyone is in the dance hall warming up with Connor. He'll put them through their paces shortly."

Just as the call was terminated, Brian's phone chirped at him again.

"Hello. Brian speaking."

"Hello Brian Speaking. Bella, here, in bellows."

"How's things down there?"

"Coping. Sid's bellows have warmed up nicely and have settled into a comfortable pattern. Do you know how long Sid's session will last?"

"I think it's about an hour, depending on his instructor. Have you heard how his pump is coping?"

"No, but I'll nip across to Piers' place if you like. Will only take me about three minutes to get there."

"Would you mind? It would be a great help. Let me know what Piers has to say."

"Will do."

*

Outside, Shane put Sid through his paces.

Having warmed up on the treadmill, Sid was directed to the shoulder press. Sitting comfortably, Sid waited while Shane adjusted the weights to allow for Sid's abilities, and when instructed he began his shoulder presses. The trainer assisted him initially, then went across the room to help someone else.

*

Back inside, Bella entered Piers' workshop to find him making notes on his clipboard while taking stress gauge readings.

"Hi Piers. Brian's just asked me to look in on you. Everything okay?"

"Yeah. All within permitted tolerances. How's things up in the bellows area?"

"Okay. I've left my 2IC in charge. I'm sure he'll phone down to me if he gets any problems, but Lee, in listening, has told me that Sid's trainer is making him take it easy for a while until he is fit enough to take things up a notch."

"That's good. With the state of Sid's pump I'm not sure he can take much punishment."

"Oh? Is there a problem. Does Brian know about it?"

"It's not too much of a problem at the moment, but he's been getting some pump murmurs and I don't want him to overdo it. Yes, Brian does know about it."

"Right. I'll get back up to my patch and let Brian know you're okay. Don't trouble to give him a report. I'll do it for you. I can see that you're busy."

"Thanks for that, Bella. Tell him I'll report any problems that might occur."

"Will do."

Bella returned to the bellows department.

*

Outside, Sid completed the fifty shoulder presses ordered by Shane and was shown to the bicycle stand.

"Fifteen minutes here, then get on the rowing machine for fifteen minutes," instructed Shane.

Sid had started to sweat while he was on the shoulder press. He was now leaking profusely. He sat on the bicycle saddle and rested for a few minutes to catch his breath.

"Don't stop now, Sid. This is the time that it's doing some good to you," barked Shane from across the room.

Everyone looked in Sid's direction so he started to pedal furiously to show them that he was not a quitter.

*

Inside, in the dance hall, everyone was also beginning to get wet. Connor, the courier and fitness manager was putting them through their own paces.

"Okay, everyone down and do fifteen push-ups. Go!"

The tiny people flopped on the floor and started to push up with arms that had never done any push-ups before. Most of them just pushed up their shoulders and bellows cage, leaving their hips and legs on the floor.

"All done? Okay, turn over and do fifteen sit-ups."

Tiny people started to groan and grumble.

"Stop grumbling and get on with it. The sooner you finish those, the sooner you can have a rest for three minutes."

Theola, the thermoregulation (aka sweat glands) manager, stood up and asked for her and her team to be excused.

"Why?" asked Connor.

"I need to take my team to monitor the thermoregulators. If Sid runs out of wetness he could overheat."

"Yes. Alright. Everyone else, carry on with your sit-ups." More groans. "Okay. Everyone…"

It was Merv's turn to interrupt Connor by waving his hand in the air.

"What is it Merv?" asked an exasperated Connor.

"Don't you think I'd better see if Brian needs me to put some ideas into Sid's ideas chip?"

"Why?"

"Well, I'd hate Brian to think that you stopped me from reporting to him"

Connor let out a long sigh. "Yes, alright. Off you go. Now…"

Billy, big wrapping manager, stood up.

"What's wrong, Billy?" with a more exasperated sigh from Connor.

"Nothing, Connor, but I've just had a thought…" Billy hesitated.

"Well, Billy?"

"Well, if Theola is going to release more wetness through Sid's big wrapping, don't you think I should be there to monitor the situation?"

There was a pregnant pause while Connor digested Billy's suggestion.

"Okay, yes. Get going." Connor was getting irritated by all the interruptions and people leaving.

Several more hands shot up and waved around for attention.

"What? What's wrong? Manny…"

"I reckon Fay from Filters, and myself should be on standby - just in case Kevin's team shoves some nourishment in our direction."

Another short pause.

"Okay, go. Nobody else is leaving! Right, everyone else raise your heels six inches and hold it." Connor scanned the room to see how many tiny people remained.

Although the remaining tiny people did as they were told, Kevin stood up and coughed for some attention.

"What now, Kevin?" Forgetting that everyone was straining to hold their heels six inches from the floor.

"If Fay and Manny are leaving to be on standby, I think I should join them - just in case Sid takes in some nourishment."

Connor stared at Kevin for all of fifteen seconds (inside world time), then answered.

"Yes. Anybody else got a flimsy excuse?"

Several more hands shot up.

With a resigned huff Connor let all those holding their hands up go. Looking round, the only tiny people left were those from his own department - all two of them. With little incentive to carry on he dismissed his staff and went to get changed.

It seems that Brian's keep fit regime was destined to fail.

*

Outside, Sid, by now, had been round all the gym equipment in the room except the rowing machine.

Sitting down, he watched as Shane tapped the keys on a small keypad in front of him to feed in the instructions regarding Sid's journey along the pretend river.

"Off you go," ordered Shane who, once more, jogged across the room to make someone else's life a misery.

Sid started to row. After about two minutes he decided that the program that Shane had tapped into the keypad was too pedestrian, so he increased his stroke. The screen in front of him showed a fictitious Sid rowing upstream, with another fictitious rowboat vying for first place to the finish line. Sid upped his game, but so did the other rower.

'*Okay,*' thought Sid, '*If he wants a race let's give him one,*' rowing harder.

The other boat had the same idea.

Now, what Sid hadn't thought of was the fact that he was competing against a computer embedded in his rowing machine's screen, and everyone knows that it's impossible to beat a computer, isn't it?

Sid rowed furiously, bettering any Olympic rower's stroke, but the finish line was still four miles away, according to the message on the screen. The faster Sid rowed, the more the computer heaped on the pressure. Sid was now going ballistic with his oars.

*

Inside, Piers was pushing buttons and pulling levers in a forlorn attempt to stabilise Sid's pump rate.

He picked up the telephone and dialled Brian.

"Tell Sid to stop what he's doing. TELL HIM TO STOP!"

Brian knew exactly what Piers was shouting about. Bella had telephoned just thirty seconds earlier to say exactly the same thing and Brian now knew that neither Sid's bellows, nor his pump, was coping with the stress of Sid's exercise.

Piers stood back to listen to Sid's pump making all sort of noises. He knew that there was nothing he could do to prevent a total shut down if Sid continued with this self destructive exercise. He dashed up the stairs to the brain department, taking the steps three at a time.

Piers crashed into the brain department at exactly the same time as Bella ran out of the lift.

With a look of horror on Brian's face he shout to Merv, "Send that message NOW Merv. GET SID TO STOP EXERCISING!".

Piers and Bella spoke up in unison. "It's too late, Brian, Sid's pump is close to shutdown, and there is nothing we can do to stop it…!"

Chapter 37
(A close call)

Sid eventually realised that his efforts to beat the rowing computer were hopeless.

There was absolutely no way that he would win this race to a pretend finish line opposing a digital competitor, so he gave up.

Sat there, sweating profusely with his chest heaving to get a good intake of breath, he felt dizzy from the effort of rowing hard. He felt his hands tingle and he watched the room begin to whorl around him. He slumped forward, onto his knees.

Shane, the personal trainer, casually looked in Sid's direction to see how he was getting on. He suddenly realised that Sid was not getting on. In fact he realised that Sid had collapsed. He dashed to the rowing machine and shouted to a neighbouring rower to help him get Sid off the equipment.

Didn't you see him collapse?" he chastised.

"What? Me? No, I was just having a race to the finish. I didn't take any notice of that bloke."

Laying Sid down, Shane felt for a pulse. There was one. A faint pulse, but a pulse, nonetheless, and this pulse was racing faster than Shane had ever felt a pulse go. Looking at his watch he timed Sid's pulse at about one hundred and seventy five beats per minute. Far too fast, and the pulse was really irregular. Shane got a low stool and placed Sid's heels on it, raising his feet above his head.

The other keep-fitters crowded round, all with a concerned look on their faces.

"Shouldn't we call for an ambulance?" someone asked.

Shane continued to monitor Sid's heartrate and answered, "Not yet. He's just overdone it on the rowing machine and fainted. He'll come round in a minute."

While the onlookers were sceptical of Shane's assessment they continued to watch for any sign of a recovery.

*

Inside, Brian and the rest of the tiny people in the brain department all stopped what they were doing and sat back to monitor Sid's brain activity.

Brian calmly said to everyone, "The servers have been overloaded with instructions and have frozen. Merv, see what you can do to defrag his memory and ideas chips. Piers and Bella, get back to your departments. I want you to report any changes in Sid's activity, especially his pump rate and oxygen intake rhythm."

The two dashed towards the lift.

Brian instructed his team. "Stay put everyone. Don't touch your keyboards until Merv has finished defragging Sid's chips. How's it going, Merv?"

"Ninety seconds," replied Merv.

Brian picked up his telephone and dialled Piers' number. "Piers, what's the situation regarding Sid's pump rate?"

"It's slowed to around one hundred and ten. It may be stabilising, but it's too soon to tell."

"Okay. Keep me informed."

Call terminated, he dialled Bella. "Bella, what's happening?"

"Sid's bellows have slowed down and are now running at about eighty-five percent. Oxygen levels are still a bit low, but they're not dangerous. All departments are receiving a diminished volume of oxygen, but enough to cope."

"Good. Stay on it."

As soon as this call was terminated the phone shouted for some attention.

"Brian…"

"Brian, this is Lee, in lookout. Sid's light shades have started to open and he is trying to focus on his surroundings. Lee, in listening, has heard what Sid's personal trainer has had to say and she understands that the trainer is monitoring Sid. Apparently he just fainted from the strain of rowing too hard. It appears that Sid is lying on his back with his feet propped up."

"Okay, Lee. Got that. Let me know if Sid's position changes and ask Lee, in listening to contact me."

"Will do."

Merv held his hand up and called out to Brian. "Memory and ideas chips all defragged, and ready to go."

Brian looked at his team, all staring in his direction and waiting for instructions.

"Re-boot your machines," he calmly instructed.

Everyone stabbed their carriage return key and watched as their PC screens all fired up and showed the welcome screen. Busily tapping in passwords the team all breathed a sigh of relief as their screens blinked onto the home pages.

"Is everyone up and running?" asked Brian, scanning the room for anyone with a problem.

Lots of thumbs were raised in answer. Only one tiny person raised a hand for some attention. Brian walked over to the tiny person's desk.

"What's the problem?" he asked.

"I'm pretty sure that lack of oxygen to his left fuel tube (*aka the internal carotid artery*) has caused the link to Sid's pump to be interrupted and damaged the source code. It looks like the source code needs some attention. I'll get on to it now, but Sid's pump will be erratic for a while until I can find where the disruption has damaged the source code."

"As quick as you can. If we can't stabilise Sid's pump the trainer will surely call for an ambulance."

"Yes, sir." The tiny operative started to tap keys to home in on the damaged line of source code.

Brian telephoned Piers to let him know about the damaged link.

"Piers, I've just been told that the link to Sid's pump got damaged when Sid overdid his exercising, hence the shut down. The source code to that link needs repairing. Are you able to keep the pump stable long enough for the repair to take place?"

"I think so. I've put the pump onto the emergency backup system but the link will need to be restored without delay. It was a close call there, for a minute or two. There was a grave danger that Sid's pump would fail completely. If that had happened, we would all have been in serious trouble."

"Yeah, got that. I think the situation is stabilising now, though. Keep me informed."

Turning to Merv, Brian instructed, "Merv, send a message to Sid's ideas chip that he is beginning to feel okay."

"Yes, sir."

*

Sid's breathing slowed and his heart rate returned to a little above normal, albeit with an erratic pulse.

Shane took a long, deep breath and said to Sid, "That was a close call, Sid. I thought we had lost you there, for a moment. What the hell were you thinking, working so hard?"

"Just got a bit carried away, that's all."

"We very nearly had to carry you away. Next time, take it a bit easier, will you? I doubt that my heart will stand the strain, and I'm certain yours won't…"

Chapter 38
(A blockage)

Several years have passed and Sid is now in his sixties.

In the intervening period, Suzy dumped Stan and hooked up with a new beau called Sonny. Sonny Summers, to be precise. He was born in January, and his name epitomises his character. Always laughing and joking and annoying Sid with his quips about Sid's expanding barrel of a stomach - Sid stopped going to the gym years ago. Suzy and Sonny got married when Suzy finished university and started work as a nurse. They now have a daughter called Sunny, after her dad. Sunny was born in October.

Anyway, back to Sid.

He and Sara decided to come down a notch or two on the holiday front. After Sid's close call on the ski slopes Sara forbid him to go near a ski boot again - ever, so they both now mingle with the toasted crowd on some sunny beach that's one thousand degrees in the shade.

Sid's health has, in fact, been no different to any other bloke his age. He's now got the usual back problems, eyesight problems and hearing problems. Like everyone else, Sid is beginning to grow old. He's not old, yet. At least, he doesn't feel old, but old age definitely *is* creeping up on him.

The tiny people inside Sid are also growing old with him.

Lee in lookout had to get Merv to send an idea to Sid's chip that he ought to go to the optician because he kept peering at the newspaper text through slitted eyes. Both Sid and Lee were both beginning to get headaches trying to focus on the words, so Lee thought it a good idea to get his eyes tested.

Likewise, with Lee, in listening. She got Merv to send Sid to get his hearing tested because he was disturbing everyone in the street with the enormously high volume of the TV. The hearing specialist recommended a hearing aid but Sid was having none of that. A hearing aid, to him, was the path to a plot in the local graveyard because "..only really old people wear hearing aids." Anyway, Sid didn't relish the idea of walking round everywhere with a hearing aid whistling at everyone because feedback caused the hearing aid to shriek out and let everyone know that Sid was wearing a hearing aid. He did, however, compromise on this, for Sara's benefit. He bought a set of Bluetooth earphones to listen to the TV. A good compromise, but it still didn't stop Sid from saying "What?" or "Pardon?" or "Speak up," when he is talking to people.

His back problem was a really good excuse not to do any more gardening. He decided to pay a local guy to do that.

You may be interested to know that Brian and Lee, in listening, never did get back together again, a rift that was noticed by the tiny people but never mentioned in public. They do, however, remain friends.

So, Sid accepted the price of growing old with dignity and he got on with life. However, he noticed the stairs in his home getting steeper everyday. He wondered if some unseen force was jacking the top step up on a weekly basis.

One thing, however, that had troubled him for some time now, was the difficulty he had trying to do a wee-wee. Not only that, the number of calls to the toilet increased, especially when he was in dreamland, head heavy on his pillow with his eyes closed to the world. In a semi-roused state he frequently had to visit the toilet in the early hours, sometimes a couple of times each night, to stare down into the toilet pan and wait for his bladder to empty. He didn't mind that as much as the lack of sleep, so he took to power napping during the day.

You may not know this but there's a tiny guy living inside everyone's body basement called Tony, the tank manager. Even Sid's got one. He is responsible for managing your tank (*aka bladder*) and ensuring that this doesn't get too full.

Now, Tony keeps in close contact with Fay in filters. She removes all the salt, toxins and waste products from Sid's nourishment and sends the resultant water (*aka pee*) down to the tank to be stored and eventually expelled via Sid's final exit chute.

Naturally, Tony also liaises closely with Eddie, the exit chutes manager because Eddie needs to be prepared for the sudden flow of water from the tank. Eddie knows that it is incredibly difficult for Sid to empty his tank if the final exit chute is inflated, so he likes to be told when Tony wants to empty the tank.

Normally, Sid's tank retains about two to three hundred millilitres of fluid (about two cupful's - outside world volume) before Tony opens the valve that allows the water to exit the tank. He's got special pressure and volume gauges that enables him to see how much water is in the tank at any given point in time. However, in times of emergency, that is to say when Sid is unable to visit a toilet, the tank can hold up to seven hundred millilitres of fluid. It's a bit of a strain because it stretches the tank sides, but it's do-able.

One thing that tends to complicate the flow of water to the final exit chute is Sid's aquarium (*aka prostate*). I mentioned Sid's aquarium way back in chapter eight.

Axel, the aquarium manager, doesn't just make sure that Sid's tadpoles are fit and healthy he ensures that the liquid inside the tank, the swimming fluid (that's seminal fluid for all you outsiders) has not gone past it's use-by date. This keeps the tadpoles swimming in a good supply of healthy fluid to help them on their way down the final exit chute and into Sara's arrival lounge.

The problem here is that sometimes the aquarium enlarges as a consequence of age or external influences (e.g. cancer). If it does enlarge it squashes the final exit chute and restricts the flow of pee to the outside.

This can be painful and, to say the least, inconvenient. No male likes to stand in front of a urinal for four to five minutes while his tank is emptied, only to find that a residue of pee always waits until he has put his final exit chute away, and zipped up his trousers, before dribbling its way out.

*

The increased toilet activity hadn't gone unnoticed by the tiny people.

Eddie, the exit chutes manager, sent an email to Brian:

INTERNAL MESSAGE

From: Eddie/exit chutes
To: Brian/brain manager

Brian,
I'm a bit concerned about Sid's discharge of
waste water.
It is taking Sid far too long to empty his tank and I
wondered if you have heard anything about it.

I've tried phoning Tony, the tank manager, but he's not answering. His phone goes straight to voice mail.

Eddie.

After reading the message Brian dialled Tony's number but he, too, was sent straight to voice mail. He turned to his runner, who was lounging in a chair, reading a book and peeling an orange.

"Connor, get off your bum and go down to the tank to see if Tony has got any problems, will you? He's not answering his phone."

"Yes, sir." Connor jumped up and ran out of the brain department.

Arriving at the tank he found Tony prodding the flexible tank walls and measuring its diameter.

"Tony, Brian sent me down here to see if you've got any problems. He's tried to phone you."

"Oh, hiya Connor. No, no real problems at the moment. Will you let Brian know that I'll send him a report shortly, when I've finished a few calculations on Sid's tank size."

Connor turned and dashed towards the stairs. Connor never takes the lift. He prefers to run up and down the stairs. That's how he stays so fit.

After relaying Tony's message to Brian he resumed his book reading and started on a fresh orange.

About half an hour later (inside world time), Brian received Tony's digital report:

REPORT

On the condition of Sid's tank

Several days ago I received a telephone call from Lee in lookout. He complained that Sid was constantly disturbing <u>him</u> in the early hours to visit the toilet. There's a bit of irony in that, don't you think? Anyway, Lee asked me if there was a problem with the tank, perhaps a leaky valve or a defective valve seal.

This morning I decided to thoroughly check this.

I could find nothing wrong with the tank's valve, seal or measuring gauges. However, I did notice that a bit of the aquarium appeared to be wrapping around the edge of its platform. A closer inspection at the rear of the aquarium confirmed that it was resting on Sid's final exit chute.

Clearly, this required further investigation.

I checked the tank's supporting cables and also the supporting platform, but could find no problem with these. One of the supporting cables seemed to be a bit tight so I loosened this to prevent it from stretching.

It may be an idea to speak to Axel about the aquarium. Something doesn't seem right with it.

End of report.

Tony.

After reading Tony's report Brian sent a message to Axel:

INTERNAL MEMO

From: Brian/brain dept.
To: Axel/aquarium

Re: Sid's waste water discharge

Axel,

I've received reports that Sid's waste water discharge is not as healthy as it should be.
Can you please inspect the aquarium and send me a report on its condition, specifically discussing why this is squashing Sid's final exit chute, and why this has not been reported to me before now?

Brian.

Axel read Brian's memo and scratched his head in puzzlement. He's never had any problems with the aquarium before, so why would it be causing trouble now?

He went to the aquarium room with his toolbox and started his inspection. Resting his toolbox on the floor he telephoned Tony, in the tank room.

"Tony? Have you been speaking to Brian about the aquarium?"

"Just a short note, Axel. I didn't go into too much detail because it's your department, but I mentioned that the aquarium seemed to be overlapping its platform at the front, and resting on the final exit chute at the back."

"Why didn't you come to me first? You know I would have looked into it straight away. Brian now thinks that I've not done my job," snapped Axel.

There was a pause while Tony composed his answer. This conversation seems to be turning a bit political, and politics is not Tony's strong point.

"Look, this issue had been raised long before Brian asked me to inspect the tank. I noticed the aquarium's anomalies while I was inspecting the tank and I suggested that Brian should speak to you about it. That's all. It wasn't my intention to drop you in it, Axel, but having seen the problem with Sid's waste water drainage I thought I should mention it to Brian. I'm sorry if he's had a go at you about it, but it does beg the question of why you haven't noticed any problem with the aquarium before now."

"Yeah, you're right, Tony. Sorry I snapped at you. I'll report back to Brian when I've finished my own inspection. It would have been nice to have received a heads up, though."

Axel terminated the call and took out his tape measure.

After spending a good hour (inside world time) inspecting every inch of the aquarium, Axel returned to his office and typed out a report for Brian:

REPORT

From: Axel/aquarium
To: Brian/brain dept.

Re: The aquarium.

As instructed, I have now finished a detailed inspection of the aquarium.
I found that the aquarium is overlapping its platform by approximately three inches at the front.
An inspection of the rear of the aquarium confirmed that it was resting on the top of Sid's final exit chute. This will probably affect Sid's discharge of waste water by restricting its flow.
There is no evidence that the aquarium has shifted position in any way. Its mountings are tight and its

central line is still perpendicular to the top of the final exit chute.

I've taken dimensions of the tank and can now confirm that it is approximately two percent larger than normal. This accounts for the overlapping at the front of the platform, and the resting on the final exit chute at the rear.

I've noticed a strange growth inside the aquarium and it is on my list to drain the aquarium down for a closer look at this.

Conclusion:

My investigations show that Sid's tank is enlarging. I have briefly discussed this with Lee, in lookout, and I understand that Sid has researched this problem.

Apparently, enlarging of aquariums sometimes happens with men of Sid's age, and his research has shown that it is likely to continue to enlarge.

There is a strange growth inside the aquarium that needs investigating.

From Sid's research, I understand that the outsiders may have a solution to this problem.

It may be appropriate for Merv to send an idea to Sid's ideas chip to get this looked into by an educated outsider.

END OF REPORT.

Axel

Chapter 39
(Wakey wakey)

At breakfast, one morning, Sara mentioned that she had been woken up, during the night, by Sid going to the toilet.

"Is everything alright?" she asked. "You've been getting up in the night for some time now."

"I don't know why, but my bladder seems to cry out for some help, usually at about three a.m. It seems to shout 'Wakey wakey', and the only thing that I can do to stop it is to go to the toilet. Another thing - I seem to be getting more and more bladder infections. I've been to see the doc twice this year, but no sooner do the antibiotics clear it up, another joins in."

"Sounds like you need to see about getting a specialist's appointment."

"Yeah. I had the same idea this morning. I'll press the doctor when I see him on Thursday."

*

Inside, Lee, in listening, made a note of the conversation between Sid and Sara and immediately sent a message to Brian:

INTERNAL EMAIL

To: Brian/brain dept.
From: Lee/listening
c.c. Tony/tank dept.

Re: Sid's tank

Brian,

I've just heard a conversation between Sid and Sara that you may be interested in. Sid has told Sara that he keeps getting tank infections and that he is going to see his educated advisor about meeting with a specialist.

Lee

Brian looked at the memo, thought about Lee's comment and telephoned Tony.

"Tony? I assume that you've read the email from Lee advising that Sid is going to see his educated advisor about his tank? Any comments?"

"Hi Brian. Yes, I have read the email. I've noticed the tank getting warmer than normal on several occasions. I haven't reported this because the tank cools down after a while. Neither have I discussed this with Daphne, the defence force manager."

"Are there any bugs in the tank, like what made Sid sick before?"

"I've noticed one or two bugs swimming around, but Sid managed to get some stuff from his educated advisor that seems to get rid of them. I think the outsiders call the bugs 'infection'. I contacted Kevin, in the kitchen, to see if Sid was eating anything that may cause this, and he tells me that Fred, the food shoveller, has been hosing some stuff from Sid's educated advisor into his kitchen chute. Stuff the outsiders call 'antibiotic'. Kevin has had to process this pronto to make way for nourishment. Anyway, the stuff seems to eradicate the bugs and calm Sid's heated tank down and it returns to its normal temperature after a while. The bugs just keep coming back. I have noticed the strange growth in the aquarium getting bigger, but I'm monitoring this until Sid's educated person can have a better idea of its purpose."

"Okay. You guys seem to have things under control, down there. Just let me know if something urgent crops up.

"Will do."

"I'll get Merv to send Sid a message to press to see a more knowledgeable guy than the doctor, urgently"

*

Outside.

Sid went to the toilet - for the third time that morning.

He was glad that the day of his doctor's appointment had arrived. Going for a pee was now becoming quite painful and that familiar stinging sensation of yet another bladder infection had returned. This time he was not going to be fobbed off with some antibiotics. He would demand to see a urologist at the local hospital.

The doctor agreed that Sid needed to see a specialist so Sid had to wait another couple of weeks before he received his appointment letter.

The day of the eagerly awaited appointment arrived – none too soon for Sid. He now had difficulty urinating, and it took him at least five minutes to empty his bladder. Even so, there was always an embarrassing dribble when he thought everything had drained out.

The urologist advised that Sid had an enlarged Prostate Gland (aka aquarium), something that Sid already knew from his doctor, and that an operation was needed to remove it, something else he also knew from his doctor.

"The hospital will let you know when to come in," informed the specialist.

Yet *another* wait for some relief, from Sid's perspective!

Chapter 40
(Sleeeeep)

At last, the day of the operation arrived and Sid made himself known to the ward receptionist.

He was given a back-to-front gown to wear, exposing his arse to all and sundry until it was tied at the back by Sara. She bundled his day clothes into a bag and sat with him until a nurse came to prep him for his operation.

The nurse made Sid lie on a trolley, covered him with a blanket and then wheeled him down the corridor towards the operating room. On the way there the nurse described in great detail what was about to happen. The narrative was interspersed with questions from Sid.

*

Inside, Lee in listening and Lee in lookout sat together in the listening department and made copious notes of the conversation and sent these up to Brian, via a runner, with a few suggestions. The notes were copied to the appropriate departments:

- *Big wrapping manager - prepare for the wrapping to be damaged in Sid's central area.*
- *All departments - Prepare to be temporarily moved to enable the outside fixer to access the aquarium.*
- *Axel - Drain down the aquarium and stand by. Send a runner to let Brian know what is happening as soon as you know.*

- *Bellows - Maintain a good supply of oxygen. Sid is probably going to stop working, so the bellows must continue to function at all costs.*
- *Brain - Prepare to shut down.*

Brian read the note and prepared the tiny people for Sid's operation. Everyone was alerted by him, via a loud message over the Tannoy system:

"ATTENTION ALL DEPARTMENTS.

THIS IS AN URGENT MESSAGE TO ALL DEPARTMENTS REGARDING AN IMMINENT SHUT DOWN OF THE SERVERS.

IT IS UNDERSTOOD BY LEE IN LISTENING THAT SID IS ABOUT TO BE WHEELED INTO THE OUTSIDER'S FIXING ROOM TO HAVE SOMETHING DONE TO HIS AQUARIUM. SOME WORK IS REQUIRED TO HELP SID SLEEP BETTER.

THE WORK, APPARENTLY, WILL STOP HIM DISTURBING EVERYONE BY PREVENTING THE NECESSITY FOR HIM TO GET UP IN THE MIDDLE OF THE NIGHT TO EMPTY HIS TANK.

ALL DEPARTMENTS ARE TO PREPARE FOR AN IMMINENT SHUT DOWN OF THE SERVERS AND THE BRAIN DEPARTMENT.

THE BRAIN DEPARTMENT WILL BE UNABLE TO ASSIST ANY OTHER DEPARTMENT UNTIL THE OUTSIDERS ARE ABLE TO RE-BOOT THE SERVERS.

ALL OTHER DEPARTMENTS SHOULD OPERATE NORMALLY.

BELLA AND PIERS, MONITOR SID'S BELLOWS AND PUMP CONTINUALLY.

SID IS PRESENTLY ON HIS WAY TO THE FIXING ROOM, SO YOU ALL HAVE JUST A FEW MOMENTS TO PREPARE.

DO NOT DELAY YOUR PREPARATIONS.

END OF MESSAGE."

There was a flurry of activity while the departments all prepared for Sid's shut-down.

*

Outside, the trolley arrived in the operating theatre (aka fixing room).

Several nurses, all wearing face masks, were busying themselves as the trolley entered the theatre. As soon as everyone was settled Sid was given an injection in the back of his hand and told to count backwards from one hundred.

He definitely remembered what came after ninety four but didn't get as far as ninety-two. His eyelids (aka shades) closed without asking and he entered the darkest, quietest room he had ever been in.

At least he wouldn't need to get up halfway through his slumber to go to the toilet...

*

Inside, everyone in the brain department sat back and waited for all of their PC monitors to go blank. When it eventually happened, the room was plunged into darkness until the emergency lighting kicked into gear.

"Okay, everyone," said Brian. "Sit tight until the server is re-booted by the outsiders. This may take a while, so I hope you have all brought some knitting to be getting on with. As soon as your screens light up please re-start your systems."

The room went quiet as the tiny people in Sid's brain department found something to do, read, knit, or just doze in their chairs.

Sid has been given an anaesthetic injection to put him to sleep and he is now attached to lots of tubes and monitors. He sleeps peacefully.

The whole of Brian's department, including Brian, has completely shut down.

The only method of communication for everyone is via the numerous staircases that link to form a network of routes to, and from, each department. The lifts, telephones and PC's (consequently all emails) are all inoperative because Sid's anaesthetic has shut down the main servers. With Brian unable to communicate properly all the departments are, in effect, now leaderless. On their own.

They do, however, continue to interact with each other and continue to work as a team.

Don't forget the reason why Sid needs to go to the fixing room. The department in the reproductive chain that is causing a lot of problems for Sid is his aquarium. His aquarium (aka prostate) is grossly enlarged and a fixer (aka surgeon) needs to look at this to see why.

The fixer, outside, finished his final checks, made sure everyone was ready and he commenced the fix.

As soon as the fixer had made the entry incision, Billy, the big wrapping manager, began sealing the nourishment tubes in the damaged area. All departments checked their furniture for stability, tied themselves down and prepared for a move. The bellows department cranked up oxygen distribution and Bella started to monitor output. Brian could do nothing except sit back and wait for the outsiders to eventually re-boot the servers.

Axel drained the aquarium. He decided that now was an ideal opportunity to see what the strange growth inside the aquarium was, and he climbed in for a closer look.

*

"Scalpel," requested the surgeon, and one was slapped into his waiting, outstretched hand.

After making his cut, he slowly and carefully eased his hand into Sid's abdominal cavity, parting the organs until he could see the prostate.

"Yes…," he said, more to himself than to the operating team, "as I thought. I'm going to have to remove his prostate," turning to his understudy.

"Feel how hard it is."

The understudy gently probed Sid's prostate. "Is there any way it can be saved?"

"No, I'm afraid not. The whole prostate will need to be taken out to prevent the cancer from spreading. Luckily, it doesn't appear to have spread anywhere else, but he will need a course of chemotherapy to be on the safe side."

Scissors were slapped into the surgeon's hand and he removed the prostate.

The understudy was left to return all Sid's inners to their correct location and sew up the temporary entry to his abdomen. Billy got to work reconnecting the nourishment tubes in the affected area.

Chapter 41
(That's what I said, sir)

Operation over, the organs (aka departments) replaced and the stomach's entry wound sewn up, Sid was wheeled into the recovery room.

"Wake up, Sid. Open your eyes for me."

These were the first words that Sid recognised as he slowly woke from his anaesthetic. His eyelids opened and he saw a nurse staring down at him.

"It's time to wake up. You're in good hands, now," the nurse reassured him.

"Yeah..." replied Sid, "That's what my wife said on our wedding night," and he started to giggle uncontrollably. He felt happy and relaxed. To the amusement of the recovery team, they joined in the laughter. They knew the reason why Sid was so jovial.

The anaesthetist had given Sid a whiff of Nitrous Oxide, otherwise known as laughing gas, to keep him calm while he recovered from the anaesthetic, and Sid wasted no time in capitalising on its effects.

*

Back inside, the servers were beginning to automatically re-boot.

The whole of the brain department, including Brian, rolled around on the floor in fits of belly laughter.

The laughing gas been pumped into to their department from the bellows and they, too, were feeling its effects. In fact, the tiny people in *every* department were rolling around, unable to contain their fits of laughter. Eventually, Brian partially composed himself and sent out a Tannoy message:

"OKAY, SETTLE DOWN EVERYONE. SID IS RECOVERING AND HE WILL NEED ALL OUR EFFORTS TO GET HIM BACK ON HIS FEET. ALL DEPARTMENTS SEND IN A REPORT ON WHAT THE OUTSIDERS HAVE DONE - Hee-Hee!"

Brian could not hold in a chuckle any longer.

One-by-one, all the servers re-booted and the departments began to settle back into their normal routines.

Lee, in listening, had a feeling of unease. She had specifically asked Axel to let Brian know what the fixers were doing, but she had heard nothing from him, or Brian. Once the phones were back on line she telephoned the aquarium department. The phone returned an unobtainable tone. Lee left it for a while, thinking that perhaps Axel's phone was not yet back on line. After about half-an-hour (inside world time) she again tried Axel's number…

Still unobtainable.

She telephoned Brian.

"Brian, this is Lee, in listening."

"Hello, Lee. Everything back up and running down there?"

"Yes, fine, but I'm phoning about Axel. Have you heard from him yet?"

"No, not yet. I've just sent Connor down to see what's going on and I'll give everyone an update as soon as I know. It's likely that Axel is still tidying up from the fixer's work. I'll call you back as soon as I can."

"Okay. Thanks."

Brian forgot about Lee's phone call because he was busy running checks on the servers with his team.

248

Some time later Connor returned from the aquarium, crashed through the doors of the brain department and shouted, "IT'S GONE! IT'S GONE! IT'S NOT THERE!"

Everyone in the department stopped what they were doing to swivel round and stare at the runner. Brian took charge.

"Alright, alright. Calm down, son. Take a breath and tell me what you think you're doing shouting and upsetting everybody with all this noise."

The runner suddenly remembered where he was, and who he was shouting at. With a deep breath he explained his panic in a shaky voice.

"You sent me down to the aquarium to find out what was happening down there."

"Yes, go on…"

"Well, sir, it's not there, and I can't find Axel anywhere. I've looked …"

Brian interrupted. "Slow down, son. One thing at a time. What's not there?"

"The aquarium, sir. It's gone!"

"The aquarium's gone? Gone where?" asked Brian in an incredulous tone.

"I don't know, sir. It's gone. Not there. The room is empty. No aquarium. It's gone."

"Did Axel tell you what he's done with it?"

"No, sir. He's not there, either!"

Brian stared at the runner for several seconds, then turned and headed for the lift.

"This way!" he ordered the runner.

"I don't use the lift, sir. I use the stairs."

"Get in…!"

The lift sank to the aquarium department and when the lift doors slid open Brian stepped into the empty room.

249

He puffed out a quick breath and said, "It's gone!"

"That's what I said, sir. It's gone."

The two men looked at each other then looked around the empty room. Brian shouted Axel's name.

"AXEL! WHERE ARE YOU?"

No reply.

Axel had disappeared with his aquarium…

Chapter 42
(So sad)

Inside, the tiny people never did find out why, or how, Axel had disappeared.

All they knew was that he was gone. Brian had ordered a complete and thorough search of all departments, but Axel was nowhere to be found. It was assumed by everyone, quite rightly, that Axel had somehow been extracted by the outsiders when they took the aquarium. Nobody considered that he had been stupid enough to climb into the aquarium at the precise moment that the surgeon had removed Sid's aquarium (aka prostate). Axel's disappearance remained a mystery to the tiny people for ever, and the event was even given a special entry in the insider's book of unusual events. The tiny people will now be able to read and puzzle over Axel's disappearance.

Forty-eight hours (outside world time) after Sid's operation, Brian summoned everyone to the place where everyone meets. They all wore their best dress, the men resplendent in their uniforms, and the women all wearing their least worn, freshly pressed dresses.

After waiting for the gathering to settle down he began, in a sombre tone, "I've asked you all here, today, to remember Axel."

Everyone looked down at the floor in silence. Some are quietly weeping, some close their eyes to remember Axel, and at least one of them took the opportunity to pick his nose.

"I'd like everyone to stand in silence, for a minute or two, while we all reflect on Axel's pride in the work that he did. Reflect on his ever smiling, joking face, and his eagerness to help each and everyone of us. He was a good man. A trustworthy man, and above all else, a friend to us all.

"He was always there to nurture and coach Sid's tadpoles. He always made sure that Sid was able to deposit the fittest and most handsomest of tadpoles into the inflated final exit chute, and Axel always kept the aquarium clean and fresh.

"With this in mind, he touched not only our lives, but also the lives of Sid and Sara, Sid's wife, and we should all celebrate the fact that their biological copy, Suzy, is the product of Axel's care and diligence.

"I am proud to have met and worked with Axel, and I am honoured to have been his friend and colleague, as I am sure we all are."

By now there were more weepy faces than dry ones. Even the bloke picking his nose pulled out his well used handkerchief to wipe the teardrops from his face, depositing something sticky on his left cheek.

After a couple of minutes of silence, occasionally interrupted by the noise of someone blowing a runny nose, Brian interrupted everyone's thoughts.

"Okay. In honour of Axel's demise, we can all take an extra day's holiday to remember him. It is up to you when you take this day, but department managers should ensure that all department tasks are covered at all times. Any questions?"

There were no questions.

"Fall out, everyone and try to get back into a normal routine."

Everyone mumbled to their neighbour as they all made their way to the exits, some still weeping, some still looking at the floor and at least one of them still picking his nose.

*

Outside, Sid laid on his back and stared at the ceiling.

While Brian was giving his eulogy, inside, Sid, for some reason, felt a bit down, himself. He didn't know why. He didn't know that that was the effect the tiny people inside him were having on his emotions, and he continued to feel down for a while even after Brian had dismissed them.

A nurse entered his ward and headed for his bedside.

"Hello, Sid. Are you feeling any better today?"

"Actually, no. I feel a bit down. A bit sad, as if a part of me has been taken away."

"It has. You've just had your Prostate removed, remember?"

"Yeah, I know, but this is more of a lethargic feeling."

"That's okay. It's normal after an operation, especially as you've come down from your whiff of laughing gas. Don't worry, it'll pass."

"Yeah, okay. What's for tea?"

Chapter 43
(Oh dear...)

You may not have noticed, but there is one tiny person that I've yet to introduce to you.

She is Sienna, the sniffer.

Sienna is Sid's smell manager and her department, the smell department, is located in Sid's Ethmoid sinus, a small area adjacent to his nasal cavity. She is responsible for several areas inside Sid's forehead, cheeks and nose (aka smell chambers), all designed to help him recognise smells, and she has an extremely important role to play in Sid's life.

Now, you may ask "Why are smells so important?"

Well, smell interacts with taste, memory and emotions. These interactions are complex, so I'm not going to bore you with the science behind them. Just know that smell alerts us to all sorts of things.

Unpleasant odours, for example, remind us what deodorant is used for. It also alerts us to the potential for the danger of something burning, say, your trousers or your hair. Conversely, it brings back childhood memories of grandma's soap, or of her delicious meat and potato pie, and it helps us to appreciate what your girlfriend's perfume smells like... Unless, of course, your girlfriend's perfume smells like wet dog, then you'll probably want to change her for a different version!

Smell also helps us to taste the nourishment that Mick the masher masticates, and Fred the food shoveller shovels down the chute to Kevin the kitchen manager.

Sometimes, however, Sienna gets inundated with work when an infection or an allergy causes swelling of the tissues lining Sid's smell chambers. Some of these areas then get blocked with snot (call it what it is…), causing congestion and some pain in Sid's face. It is her job to clean up the mess left by the snot after the infection has been eradicated by Daphne, the defence force (aka immune system) manager.

Sienna is a busy lady at any time of the day or night so she doesn't get much time to socialise… Not until Brian visits for an 'inspection' of her department, anyway.

Yep! You've got it. After Lee, in listening, dumped Brian during a misunderstanding at dinner, one evening, Brian made a move towards Sienna, not least because she smells nice.

They meet up in Sienna's changing room in Sid's frontal sinus (aka top smell chamber) for his 'inspections' after an email with a hidden message has been sent by one of them. Brian and Sienna think that their regular 'inspections' are secret, but everyone has put two-and-two together and cottoned onto the fact that Brian's frequency of smell chamber inspections is obvious, not least because somebody in Sienna's department caught them canoodling… And blabbed.

*

Outside, it is two-thirty in the morning.

Sid and Sara are sleeping peacefully, heads nestled in their pillows, arms draped over each other's torso.

Sid dreamt of his younger days. Days when he and his friends played cowboys and Indians in the fields surrounding his home. Days when his dad took him fishing, and days when he buried his mum up to her neck on a sandy beach whilst on holiday in some sunny foreign country (The police had to dig her out quickly because the tide was coming in!).

Sid was well and truly down the dark tunnel of slumber, oblivious to any goings on around him.

I'm going to digress from Sid's dreams for a short time while I give you a quick lesson on fire.

No, not "FIRE!" as in "pull that lanyard to fire the cannon for a twenty-one gun salute," or "You're fired!" - no explanation necessary - but fire, as in "Phew! That's hot!"

It's important...

In order for fire to get going, it needs three things: oxygen, heat and fuel.

Although oxygen surrounds us, and we breathe it in, it can be generated by other means, such as a chemical reaction, or by ventilation from an open door or window, or from a scuba diving bottle.

The second of fire's needs is heat. Without a source of heat, say, rubbing two sticks together... I did this when I went camping in my younger days and it's bloody hard work... Anyway, without a source of heat you cannot have any fire. Matches, or a cigarette lighter or a blow-torch are effective as a source of heat, and they're infinitely less work than rubbing two sticks together.

The third, fuel, is equally as essential as the first two. Fuel for the fire can be paper, chemicals, wood, gas, or anything that is flammable.

So, you need these three things to start a fire and get warm.

Now, in terms of house fires, these can happen at any time of the day but are most common between the hours of six p.m. and eight p.m. House fires ignite least between the hours of four a.m. and six a.m.

257

Final words of warning are that fire is fast. In the space of thirty seconds a small flame can expand to a major fire. It takes just a few minutes for fire to engulf a whole house. Fire is hot. Room temperatures in a fire can reach one hundred degrees at floor level and rise to six hundred degrees at eye level. Inhaling this super-hot air will scorch your lungs and melt clothes to your skin. And fire is deadly. Smoke and toxic gases kill more people than flames do, and the poisonous gases created by fire can, and will, make one disoriented and drowsy.

There… Lesson over, let's get back to Sid's dream state.

Sid's dream has morphed into a full blown chase by him through the streets of some unrecognisable town. There isn't enough data to say who Sid is chasing where, and why, but suffice to say that he and Sara are both in the final sleep state, Stage four; slow-wave sleep (SWS).

This is the deepest stage of sleep, when brain activity is at its lowest and one's body is recovering, enhancing bone and muscle development. If you are in the middle of the SWS stage, it is usually difficult to wake up.

Inside, when a person enters the SWS stage all departments are reduced to a skeleton night staff.

Earlier that evening, Sara tried to make a call on her mobile phone. She heard a bleep when she turned the phone on, then it went dead, no doubt in its final SWS stage. She peered at the screen. No bars in the charge icon.

"Blast!" Sara muttered.

She looked around for her charging plug and cable but it was nowhere to be seen.

Okay, I'm going to go off-piste (so to speak) again, just for a second.

Some people believe that there is no such thing as an 'accident'. They don't believe that accidents 'just happen'. These people reckon that an 'accident' is the result of someone's negligent, or inattention. Most vehicle 'accidents', for example, occur because some buffoon is texting on his phone while driving, or a woman is concentrating more on the kiddy-fight in the back seat of her car than she is on the road ahead.

Anyway, these no-accident believers will say that an 'accident' is more the result of a set of bizarre circumstances, any one of which could, in the first place, have been avoided if someone had taken the time and effort to *think* about what they were doing.

I've said this before, and I'll say it again. "People are stupid!"

It's true...

A man, reading his morning paper will *think* that he has put his mug of hot tea safely on the table in front of him - without looking 'cos he's reading about some idiot politician who got caught with his trousers down - but he put the mug just halfway on the table's edge. Stupid, or what? The mug tips over the edge of the table and the bloke gets his trousers, and leg, doused in hot tea. An 'accident'? He would argue that it was. The no-accident believers would say "No! Not an accident. Inattention and stupidity." The circumstances, they would say, are: (1) The guy is reading his paper and not paying attention to where the table is. (2) He placed the mug on the edge of the table and not firmly on its surface - Stupid, eh? (3) The mug tips off the edge, spilling his tea all over him. Oops! Get the point?

Anyway, back to Sara's mobile phone.

Circumstance number (1) - Sara's phone ran out of juice.

"Sid, can you pass me your phone charger, please?" she asks. Without thinking, Sid passes his phone charger to Sara. He assumed that she was being helpful by plugging *his* phone in to the charger, and his attention was focused on the TV. That was the last he thought about his phone charger. Circumstance number (2) - Sid's inattention.

Now, there's a subtlety in the style of charger used for Sid's phone to the one for Sara's. A difference so subtle that Sara doesn't see it, not that she looked, or even asked, in the first place. The charger that Sid uses is a fast-charger type, a type that Sara's ancient phone battery is not designed to use.

Sara jammed the phone end of the charging cable into the phone and plugged the opposite end into the wall. With that, she put the phone on the settee arm to charge up for her phone call... And forgot about it. Circumstance number (3) - Wrong phone charger. Sara thought that the charger was the type that could be used with any phone. A wrong call (no pun intended).

In the course of the evening, the phone slowly slid down the arm of the settee and nestled into the space between the settee arm and seat cushion - unseen and forgotten by Sara. Circumstance number (4) - Sara's inattention allowed the phone to disappear down the side of the settee arm.

At ten forty-five p.m. Sid turned off the TV and he and Sara went to bed. Sara's phone began to warm up. Circumstance number (5) - Because the phone charger is a fast-charger type the ancient phone was unable to cope with the sudden influx of power and it began to overheat.

Mobile phones have been known to self ignite for several reasons, but the most common problem is excessive heat. If a charging battery becomes too hot too quickly, it can ruin the chemical makeup of the phone's components and a chain reaction, called thermal runaway, can cause the battery to generate even more heat... And eventually catch fire or explode.

Oh dear! A set of five bizarre circumstances occurred and caused Sara's phone to overheat, catch fire and put both her and Sid in immanent danger!

Chapter 44
(What's that smell?)

Cut back to two forty-five in the morning.

Outside, Sara's phone has overheated and self ignited.

Within minutes, the settee was fully ablaze and the room temperature rapidly climbed to three hundred degrees Celsius. The heat was such that all the furnishings and carpet in the room quickly self ignited.

Sid and Sara slept peacefully.

As thick, black smoke filled the room the temperature at ceiling height reached the optimal six hundred degrees to create a flashover.

A flashover is a simultaneous ignition of the combustible materials in an enclosed area.

When soft, organic materials are heated (e.g. furniture cushions), they undergo thermal decomposition and release flammable gases. Flashover happens when the flammable gases reach their autoignition temperature, usually at ceiling height, and self combust.

It didn't take long for the fire to spread to the adjacent room and make its way towards the staircase. Suffocating smoke preceded the fire, which curled its way up the staircase and collected at ceiling level outside Sid and Sara's bedroom. As more smoke was pushed upstairs by the heat, the hall, stairs and landing quickly became impassable. To make matters worse, the fire downstairs increased in severity when the lounge windows exploded and let in more oxygen for the fire to feed on.

As the volume of hot smoke at the top of the stairs increased, wisps of smoke began to percolate under the bedroom door.

Sid and Sara still slept peacefully.

*

Inside, at two-fifty a.m. (outside world time) Sienna's 2IC thought she could smell something burning.

She turned to her colleague and asked, "What's that smell?"

The co-worker sniffed, stuck his nose in the air, sniffed again and replied, "No, can't smell anything."

The 2IC wasn't convinced by her co-worker's response. "Look after things while I go up to lookout."

The co-worker shrugged, acknowledged the 2IC's instruction and looked puzzled as the 2IC made her way to the lift. "Don't get caught bunking off," he smiled.

The 2IC ignored the comment.

Up in lookout, Sienna's 2IC approached Lee's 2IC and asked "What's that smell?"

Lee's 2IC looked around the room, sniffed, looked up, sniffed again, looked back at Sienna's 2IC and sniffed again. "Nope. Can't smell anything."

"There's something burning. I know there is."

The lookout operative pointed to the shades (aka Sid's eyelids), shrugged his shoulders dispassionately and declared, "Can't look out until Sid opens the shades."

Sienna's 2IC took in a deep breath of frustration, turned and headed, once more, towards the lift.

"Let me know if you find anything," the lookout chap said in a matter-of-fact tone as he watched the back of Sienna's 2IC's head disappear into the lift.

Sienna's 2IC ignored that comment, as well.

Back down in the smell department it is now three a.m. (outside world time). The fire is now raging in the lounge downstairs and thick smoke is beginning to curl its way upstairs.

Sienna's 2IC asked her colleague if he could smell anything yet.

"Nope. Not a thing. Do you want me to turn up the sensitivity indicator?"

"Haven't you done that, yet?" looking at the PC screen. "Do it now. Sensitivity needs to be one hundred percent."

"Seems a bit high for nothing," the colleague said after blowing out a lung full of indifference.

"Do it…!" demanded the 2IC, "…and the next time you speak to me like that I'll put you in front of Brian so fast your feet won't touch!"

The workman stiffened up, looked at the 2IC with wide, surprised eyes and snapped back, "Yes Ma'am."

With a sense of urgency he adjusted the smell sensitivity indicator, as instructed, and stood back to let the 2IC see the PC screen. The indicator needle slowly crept up and hovered just short of the orange sector.

It is now five minutes past three and the choking smoke is filling the landing ceiling outside the bedroom door. Sienna's 2IC took another deep sniff into her lungs. Still the same as before. She picked up the telephone handset and dialled Sienna's room number.

After a few seconds, Sienna answered. "Yes, what is it?"

"Sienna, I'm sorry to disturb you, but can you please come to the control room? I think we may have an incident to manage."

"What kind of incident?"

"I think I can smell something burning."

There was a pause as Sienna absorbed her 2IC's comment, then she replied, "Are you sure?"

"No, Ma'am, I'm not sure, but I've got a strong feeling that something bad is going to happen."

Sienna never doubted her 2IC's judgement, that's why the 2IC was promoted to 2IC.

"Okay, give me a minute to put some clothes on."

It is now seven minutes past three and the landing is rapidly filling with thick, grey smoke, swirling around and looking for somewhere to go.

Sienna entered the smell department control room at three-twelve a.m. and approached the PC console.

"Have you detected anything, yet?" she asked.

"No Ma'am," answered the 2IC, "but the sensitivity indicator has just entered the orange sector."

"Yes, there's definitely something going on," declared Sienna, peering at the PC screen.

Suddenly, they all felt an immediate waft of unexpected air pressure as the windows downstairs exploded and the fire sucked in more oxygen.

"Did you feel that?" asked Sienna, and everyone in the room nodded.

Smoke began to curl up from under the door of the department's control room and the sensitivity dial needle shot round to the red zone. Alarm bells started to ring loudly and red flashing lights lit up the control room and department's sleeping quarters.

All the tiny people in the smell department were roused by the noise and rude awakening of the alarm lights. They all jumped out of bed and quickly began pulling up trousers, buttoning up blouses and pushing shoes onto their feet.

They all asked the same question.

"What's that smell?"

Chapter 45
(Jump!)

Lee's 2IC, in listening, heard the crash of shattering glass as the lounge window exploded.

"What was that?" he asked the night shift listening team.

They all looked round at each other, then returned to their screens. One of them alerted him to a screen showing a graph line something akin to that shown on an outsider's PC screen when an earthquake has just taken place somewhere.

The 2IC stared at the squiggly line and picked up the telephone to dial his boss's number.

Lee, the listening manager, always slept lightly. She felt the jolt as the room vibrated and opened her eyes when the window exploded. She was already out of bed and pulling up knickers when the telephone rang.

"Speak!" she ordered.

"Lee, we've just heard something crash and one of our screens shows an anomaly in the soundwaves. It's not what you would expect at this time of the night."

"Yes, I felt the vibration. I'm on my way. Telephone Lee in lookout. Ask if Sid has opened his shades."

Lee's 2IC, in lookout, was oblivious to what was happening elsewhere, although he also felt the tremor when the lounge window exploded. Peering into his enormous binoculars he saw that Sid had not yet opened the shades. Sid was clearly still fast asleep. His conversation with Sienna's 2IC unnerved him and he picked up his lookout manual to search for the procedure for an event such as this.

Lee in listening entered a chaotic department. Staff were also flicking through pages of their manuals to find the correct procedure. She approached her 2IC.

"What's the situation?"

"Not a lot has changed since I telephoned you. Sid appears to be sleeping soundly, as if nothing happened."

"Have you determined what that crash was?"

"No, Ma'am."

Suddenly, the silence was shattered as the emergency alarm shrieked and a flashing red light lit up the department. In fact EVERY department was aroused by the emergency sirens and flashing red lights.

Brian jumped out of bed, squirmed into his dressing gown, pushed on his slippers and dashed to the brain department.

"What's going on?" he demanded as he entered the control room.

His 2IC answered, "Don't know, yet, but it seems that all departments have been alerted to something going on outside."

The telephone rang.

"Brian, brain department," he answered.

The call was from Sienna, in smell. "Brian. There's a fire outside but Sid and Sara are unaware of it. They're still asleep! We've got smoke percolating under our door so it must be bad."

"Okay. Thanks Sienna. I'm on it."

Turning to Merv who was, by this time, sat at his console in his jim-jams and slippers, Brian ordered, "Merv, send an urgent message to Sid's wake-up chip to boot up all servers. He needs to open his eyes... NOW!

Every department inside Sid was now fully awake, alerted by the sirens and flashing lights, and all standby personnel were quickly getting dressed and dashing to their respective departments, ready to receive their orders.

In the smell department the room was rapidly filling with smoke.

Sienna's 2IC observed, "If Sid doesn't wake up soon we're going to have to abandon the department.

"Not yet," answered Sienna. She turned to face her colleagues. "Everyone stay calm and continue to monitor what Sid whiffs. We must be ready for when Brian eventually wakes him."

With handkerchiefs pushed to their mouths and noses, the smell department staff returned to their PC screens.

Brian issued an order to all departments over the Tannoy.

"EVERYONE! WE MUST WAKE SID FROM HIS DEEP SLEEP. MERV'S MESSAGE TO HIS WAKE-UP CHIP HAS NOT TAKEN ANY EFFECT, SO WE MUST ALL SHOUT TO HIM TO WAKE UP. NOW!"

Everyone in every department started shouting and screaming "WAKE UP, SID! WAKE UP SID!"

*

Outside, Sid stirred.

His dream had been disturbed by the sound of people shouting at him. He couldn't tell what, exactly, had been shouted or by who, but he was disappointed that his dream of floating in the warm waters of an ocean, somewhere, had been cut short. Maybe it was his bladder shouting to go to the toilet, again?

Still extremely sleepy, he half opened his eyes to see that it was three-fifteen in the morning, according to his bedside clock.

"Oh, well," he thought, "I suppose I'd better go."

He was now beginning to wake up and just as he swung his legs out of bed he smelled the smoke that had percolated under his bedroom door and filled the room. Suddenly he was fully awake! He swiftly turned on his bedside lamp, and immediately realised that the room was filling with thick, choking smoke.

Turning to Sara, he tried to rouse her... Nothing!

He shook her again. "Sara! Wake up!" he shouted. Still nothing.

He could sense that the smoke in the bedroom was getting thicker - and hotter!

"SARA! WAKE UP!" violently shaking her shoulder. Still nothing.

He quickly felt for Sara's pulse. There was one. A faint one, but a pulse, nonetheless. It was clear to Sid that she was now unconscious from the effects of the choking smoke. Somehow, he had to get her out of the room. Into fresh air. Away from this smoke.

Turning to look at the bedroom door he saw flames licking their way under it. It was obvious that an exit via the landing was out of the question. There was only one route available to him.

He opened the bedroom window and a blanket of thick black smoke immediately escaped through it.

Mustering all the strength that was available to him he roughly picked Sara up from the bed and made his way to the window. Getting Sara out of the window wasn't easy, but he eventually managed to get her onto the conservatory roof. The flames were now eating their way along the carpet towards the bed. It wouldn't be long before the bed was consumed, and the temperature in the room was now unbearable.

Quickly climbing out of the window he saw several of his neighbours gathered in the rear garden, some with buckets of water trying to douse the flames through the lounge window, others waiting with blankets and watching as Sid fought to get Sara away from the bedroom window, flames now beginning to lick at the window frame inside the bedroom.

"JUMP!" they shouted. "JUMP!"

He picked Sara up, once more, carried her to the edge of the conservatory roof and jumped, with Sara in his arms and with as much force as his legs would allow.

The neighbours didn't catch either of them. They didn't need to. Both Sid and Sara landed with a huge splash in Sid's swimming pool.

Sara was dragged out of the pool by the neighbours and put into a waiting ambulance where a paramedic immediately began to work on her. Firemen busied themselves with axes and fire hoses as Sid was wrapped in a neighbour's blanket.

Five minutes later, what remained of Sid's home suddenly collapsed into a heap of burning rubble.

Sid joined Sara in the ambulance as the doors were about to close.

"She'll be okay…," advised the paramedic as Sara's nose and mouth was carefully wrapped in an oxygen mask. "…she's beginning to come round."

*

Brian and the rest of the tiny people inside Sid all breathed a sigh of relief as they heard the good news, from both

Lee in listening and Lee in lookout, that Sid and Sara were okay.

Brian, particularly, was pleased as he reflected on the fact that Sid's tiny army had all worked together to wake Sid up before it was too late.

Piers, the pump manager, did not, however, celebrate with the rest of the tiny people. He was struggling to stabilise Sid's pump rate… Again!

Chapter 46
(It's time, Sid...)

I'm going to jump forward to the year 2067. Sid is eighty years old.

He's had a somewhat eventful life, but he's enjoyed every hour of it... Every hour, that is, except one. That was the hour that Sara had a fatal stroke two years ago. Sid was unable to revive her. She was rushed to hospital with Sid in the back of a speeding ambulance but, unfortunately, nobody could revive her. She died long before the ambulance arrived at the emergency department. Despite every effort by the paramedic to revive her, during that memorable journey, Sid watched Sara's life ebb away, unaware that all the really, really tiny people inside Sara had joined her on that final journey to somewhere eternally peaceful. I bet they had a party to remember when they arrived there...

Sid was sad, of course, but he took comfort in the fact that he and Sara had enjoyed sixty years of happy marriage. A greater consolation for him was the loving daughter, three grand-children and two great grand-children that had all shared their lives with him and Sara. He was proud in the knowledge that they would all grow old remembering Grandma, her wonderful cooking - especially her legendary cherry trifle - and her perpetual smile.

Do you remember Suzy's husband, Sonny Summers? He is now a world famous author, with twelve books - eight of them best sellers - and he has been able to purchase a big house on lots of acres for all his family. All eight of them. His daughters, Sunny and Shiny, and his son, Sonny Jnr. (after his dad), and his daughter's children, Sonny III (after his dad), Suzy (after her grand-mum) and, of course... Sid.

In his earlier years Sid spent a lot of time romping in those acres of land with his 'tribe', as he likes to call them, camping out with them in the summer and building a huge snowman in the winter. But his frailty now prevents such energetic activities. He watches as Suzy and Sonny camp out with their children in the summer, and throw snowballs at them in the winter. Much to Sid's delight, they sometimes 'gang up' on him and shower him with snowballs as he sits on the porch, watching everyone laughing in carefree abandonment.

*

Inside, Sid's tiny army has also grown old.

They, too, have seen Sid's family grow up around him and they have shared his joys and, of course, his sorrows. Brian held a memorial service for Sara in the room that everyone gathers, at the same time as her funeral service outside. The dialogue from the outsider's minister and music from the outsider's church was relayed to them over the Tannoy system by Lee in listening. There wasn't a dry eye anywhere in the room, but life goes on for the tiny people. It has to. They've never been afforded the time to fully relax because Sid's organs have needed constant care and attention for the whole of his life, but they have survived every one of Sid's ups and downs.

The tiny army now spends much of its time repairing the things that break down when one gets old.

Brian fights to keep the servers running. Merv constantly cleans Sid's memory chips in the hopes that Sid will retain his memory. A hopeless task, but he sticks at it. Lee, in lookout, has difficulties in focusing on the newspaper and Lee, in listening, has almost given up trying to record conversations between Sid and his family. Mick, the masher, and Fred, the food shoveller, now work together to sweep and hose into the chute the pulped dinner that Sid spoons into his mouth because he no longer has any teeth.

Everyone inside now has a daily battle to keep Sid's systems running smoothly.

One tiny person, in particular, has fought for many years to keep the nourishment running through Sid's nourishment tubes. Piers, the pump manager.

This morning, Piers sat at his console and watched as Sid's pump rate became abnormally unstable.

Piers has had to nurse Sid's pump for years. Most of the time the pump rate has been stable, but occasionally some extra physical work has made the pump struggle to maintain its regularity. The pump rate at those time runs inconsistently, sometimes running too fast, sometimes running too slow, and Piers has had to do some out-of-the-box thinking to stabilise it. Generally, such anomalies have not bothered Sid. He usually put his irregular heart beat down to "too much hard work," but Piers has seen his pump gradually decline in efficiency over the years.

Right now, though, the pump has unexpectedly increased in speed. Piers telephone Brian.

"Brian, do you know if Sid is exercising?"

"No, why?"

"His pump rate has accelerated without any prompting from me. Do you know if there's a problem outside?"

"Not to my knowledge. I'll phone Lee in lookout to ask if he's seen anything."

Call terminated, Brian phoned Lee in lookout.

"Lee, have you seen Sid doing any exercise today?"

"No, Brian. His shades are down so I assume he's still asleep. Is there a problem?"

"Don't know, yet. I'll get on to Lee in listening and speak to you again later."

As soon as Brian returned the handset, the department lights on his telephone began to light up.

Picking up the handset, Brian stabbed the button to connect the call from Tommy, the temperature manager.

"Brian, I'm a bit concerned. Sid's temperature is rising, but there doesn't seem to be any reason for it. Lee in lookout tells me that Sid appears to be resting."

"Okay, Tommy. I'm aware that there is some kind of a problem with Sid at the moment but I haven't been able to isolate it yet. Stand by."

Brian turned to Connor.

"Connor, phone round all the departments and let them know that I am aware of a problem with Sid and that I'm working on it. Tell them to stop phoning me. I need a communication line to find out what the problem is."

"Yes, sir."

Connor doesn't run anywhere nowadays. The stairs are too much for him. Instead he has been provided with a telephone of his own to communicate Brian's instructions.

Brian phoned Piers.

"What's the situation?"

"Not too good. The pump rate is racing and I'm unable to control it. It doesn't look good for Sid right now."

"Okay, keep at it and keep me informed."

"Will do."

Piers returned to his consol and continued his quest to slow Sid's pump rate down.

*

Outside, Sid slept.

It is eleven-thirty in the morning and it is unusual for Sid to sleep so late. Suzy poked her head around his bedroom door to check on him. She worried about his frailty. How slow he had become when he shuffled from one room to another. How forgetful he was and how he was eating less at each meal. He told her that he just didn't feel like much to eat nowadays, but he always complimented her on the delicious spread that she put out. She worried at how he had begun to sleep in later, and later, each day. However, she accepted that growing old comes with many changes, and she never made a fuss over the things about him that worried her.

Sid, on the other hand, has never accepted that he has grown old. He perseveres at everything he does, whatever the task, never giving in to his frailty. His efforts are sometimes accompanied with a few ripe words, but his family accept his ways and they thank God that Sid has not succumbed to the evils of dementia. The children marvel at his ability to still be able to dress himself and they all laugh at his perpetual jokes and amusing derision of their parents.

It is now eleven forty-five and Sid is still asleep.

He dreamt of Sara and himself lazily walking across a beautiful green field with daisies and dandelions looking upwards towards the heavens. Poppies and buttercups have pushed through the lush, green carpet of grass to drink in the warmth of the spring sun, and clover parades its pink and purple flowers to entice the bees and butterflies to its sweet nectar.

The two lovers talk about nothing in particular. They reminisce about their childhoods, and about Suzy's childhood, and about the grand-children's childhoods. They amused themselves trying to guess what their grand-children will grow up to be; a doctor, or an engineer, or a chef, or somebody famous. Idyllic words in an idyllic place somewhere far away from the crowds, in an idyllic world.

Sara stopped walking and looked at Sid as he took a few more steps before realising that his beloved Sara was not at his side. Turning to face her, he saw that she had that perpetual smile on her face that greets everyone she sees.

"What?" Sid asked.

Sara stood and smiled that everlasting, appealing, beautiful smile. The smile that he never forgot. He walked up to her.

"What's wrong?" he asked

Quietly and softly, still smiling, Sara replied, "It's time, Sid…"

"No… No, no, no. Not until I've said goodbye to my family…," tears welling up in his eyes.

As Sara dimmed into a haze of sunlight Sid heard her say "I'll wait here for you."

She disappeared, leaving Sid to shout, "Not yet! Not yet!"

Suzy heard Sid's cries of "Not yet!" while she was ironing downstairs in the utility room. She quickly turned the iron off and dashed upstairs to see what Sid was shouting about.

Entering his bedroom she noticed that he was still asleep. At least, he *appeared* to be asleep.

She checked his pulse - fast and irregular, but still there. She tried to wake him - no response. After several attempts to rouse him she decided that it was useless to continue and she dialled the emergency number to call for an ambulance, tears streaming down her own cheeks. She couldn't help noticing that Sid had also been crying.

*

Inside, Lee, in listening, was beginning to panic. Despite being asked not to by Brian's runner, she dialled Brian.
"Brian. I'm really worried about Sid. I've just heard Suzy trying to wake him up, but he is unresponsive, Suzy has telephoned for an ambulance."
"Yes, I've just had a conversation with Piers and it seems that Sid's pump has just had a setback. A big one. Piers is trying to stabilise it."
"Is it serious, Brian?"
"Don't know, yet, but it doesn't look good. Got to go - I've got a call coming in from Lee in lookout. It looks like Sid's shades have dropped on their own. I'll call you back when I can."

Piers has run out of ideas - and breath. All he could do now was to sit back and watch as Sid's pump fluttered uncontrollably. It settled down on its own, but became weaker as each moment passed.

*

Outside, there was a knock on Suzy's front door. Her daughter answered the knocking.
"Mum, there's a paramedic wanting to come in."
"Yes, yes," shouted Suzy, "send him upstairs, quickly."

The paramedic put his motorbike helmet on the floor and dashed up the stairs to find Suzy waiting outside Sid's bedroom door.

"He's in here," she said, indicating inside the bedroom with an outstretched hand.

They both entered the room and the paramedic got to work immediately, stethoscope being pushed into his ears and a thermometer being placed in Sid's armpit.

Suzy and her daughter felt helpless as they watched the paramedic busily expose Sid's chest and listened to his heart. He then took out a syringe and injected Sid with something retrieved from his bag of tricks. Standing back, he continued to listen to Sid's heart. After a while he stood upright, unplugged his stethoscope from his ears and continued to hold Sid's wrist to monitor his pulse. He turned to Suzy.

"I'm afraid he has just had a heart attack," he said, solemnly. He pressed a button on his radio and confirmed that an ambulance is required. Turning back to Suzy he continued, "I've managed to stabilise the Arrhythmia, but he will need to go to hospital. The ambulance is on its way."

Suzy phoned round her family and let them all know what had happened, and where Sid was being taken. While she waited for the ambulance to arrive she packed a few things in a holdall for herself. She knew that this hospital trip could be several days long.

*

Back inside, Brian looked at the carnage in the server room. Twenty five of the thirty servers were well and truly out of action. Some of them were smoking, others just lifeless.

He turned to his 2IC.

"How bad is it?" he asked.

"As bad as it gets, Brian. Only five servers are working, and three of those are overheating. I don't have any more spares."

"Well, I'd better summon everyone to the meeting room to give them the bad news."

Brian turned and walked, head down, towards the Tannoy microphone. He knew that he had a hard and difficult task to explain the situation to the tiny army, and he sadly pondered over what words he would need to say.

*

Outside, a couple of hours later, Suzy collected all of Sid's family in the hospital's family room to give them the news.

"I'm afraid that granddad has had a very bad heart attack. It's difficult to say whether he will survive, but the doctors are doing everything to keep him alive. We'll just have to wait here until we are told what's happening."

The children started to cry and everyone huddled in a sorry circle to await whatever news can be brought to them.

After a while, a doctor entered the room and approached Suzy.

"We've done as much as we can to make Sid as comfortable as possible," he advised, "but I'm afraid that he doesn't have very long to live. Perhaps now would be a good time for you all to say your goodbyes to him."

With that, he left the family alone to compose themselves for their final words with Sid.

They were shown to a private ward where Sid laid in bed. He was half awake, his eyelids lazily opening and closing, as if he had difficulty in keeping them open. He looked round at his family and smiled, gently.

"Don't cry," he said to the children, in a voice barely audible. "When you've gotta go, you've gotta go," he remarked in his usual jovial tone.

Nobody was amused.

The children crowded round his bed and held on to anything that resembled an arm, or a hand. As Suzy and Sonny looked on, Suzy gently held his cheek in the palm of her hand, her teardrops falling onto Sid's shoulder.

"I love you all," muttered Sid.

"We all love you," responded Suzy.

Sid smiled a warm and gentle smile at her, and said, "It's time…"

Surrounded by his family, Sid closed his eyes and waited for his beloved Sara to meet him on that field of lush green grass, with the daisies and dandelions, and poppies and buttercups, and clover parading its pink and purple flowers to entice the bees and butterflies.

Epilogue

The room inside where all the tiny army has congregated for years is now full.

Everyone is quiet.

The throng of tiny people is subdued, everyone looking around the room, and speaking in hushed tones. Somebody coughed a muffled cough, but no-one paid any attention.

"What's this about?" whispered Kevin to his neighbour. The neighbour looked back and just shrugged his shoulders.

The woman in front of Kevin turned and responded, "I heard a rumour that there's a problem with Sid, but I don't know what."

Brian entered the room, hand in hand with Sienna. They had married several years ago.

He stood behind the podium and waited for everyone to settle down. A silence descended on the crowd that was deafening. He looked at Sienna as if to search for an opening to his address to the tiny people and she placed a comforting hand on his arm. He turned a tearful face to the tiny people, all looking up at the stage and silently waiting for him to speak.

Blowing his nose loudly into a hanky provided by Sienna, he started the hardest speech that he has ever had to make in his life.

"You've no doubt heard that Sid has got a problem. A big problem. You may also have noticed that Piers, the pump manager, is not present. He is helping the outsiders with Sid's pump, so you will perceive that Sid's problem is very much related to his pump…"

He paused to let his first words sink in. The tiny people all looked at each other without speaking.

"… His failing pump," continued Brian.

Another pause to let those words sink in. Sienna moved closer to Brian and hooked an arm around his.

Brian interrupted everyone's mumbled discussions. "This morning, Piers reported that Sid's pump was beginning to act abnormally. Suzy also noticed this and she phoned the outsider's emergency number for some help. Sid was taken into the outsider's repair building and educated outsiders were summoned to Sid's bedside. Lee, in listening, reported that an educated outsider has told Suzy that Sid is about to stop working… Permanently."

Everyone now spoke out aloud to each other, asking questions that nobody could answer. Some began to cry - those that had absorbed the enormity of Brian's words. Brian gave the crowd a few seconds to digest his words, then interrupted the discussion, once more.

"I have to say that what Lee heard validates my own assessment of Sid's status because the brain servers are gradually shutting down. At this stage, I have no idea how long I can keep the servers working, but I am sure that you all now realise what will happen to us when the final server ceases its output."

The tiny people resurrected their previous conversations with their neighbours. Brian detected a feeling of panic spreading throughout the throng. He had to bring some order back into the proceedings.

"Quiet! Quiet!" he ordered. Everyone stopped talking and silence, once more, descended on the room.

"You've all been made aware of this moment each time you have attended my lectures on Sid's status, and it should not be a surprise to any of us. After all, Sid…"

Brian corrected himself. "… We…, have grown old with Sid and we all know that nothing lasts forever."

Everyone nodded in agreement. More mumblings, and more tiny people started to cry.

Someone broke the silence to ask, "What is to become of us?"

Silence descended on the room like a dark cloud, cloaking the room in its heavy weight.

Brian thought about the question for a long time, then answered, "That is the question that the outsiders have been striving to answer since the beginning of time. They don't know, and I'm afraid that I don't know, either. Nobody knows the answer to that."

This time the silence persisted. Everyone looked up at him, their faces searching for some words of comfort from him. Brian could see that his army of tiny people were now worried about their futures. Frightened, even. He looked at Sienna for some inspiration. She smiled and squeezed his arm in encouragement.

Turning back to the assembly, he said, "Look… Let's not dwell on what happens next. Let's all remember the good times that we've helped Sid enjoy. And let's not forget that Sid could never have survived in the first place had it not been for all you people working together."

He felt the mood lift as the tiny people started to talk amongst themselves, reminiscing about what they had done to make Sid's life enjoyable.

Brian jumped on the chance to lift the mood even further.

"Without your teamwork, Sid would have had many, many more problems than he has had in his lifetime. Bella, you have worked with Piers to maintain a good oxygen supply to Sid's nourishment tubes. Piers has relentlessly nursed Sid's pump for years. Kevin, you have worked with Fay and Manny to send the nourishment up to Bella. Fay, you have worked with Tony to keep his nourishment clean and Tony, you have always ensured that Sid's tank is emptied in a timely way.

"What about Mick and Fred? You two have laboured hard to send Sid's food down the chute to Kevin in a state that he can process easily… and Blaire - Let's not forget how Blaire has worked with Edgar and Eddie to send Sid's healthy tadpoles to Sara's arrival lounge… And don't forget Axel. Remember Axel, the aquarium manager? He always made sure that Sid's tadpoles were well trained and fit for their journey to Sid's inflated final exit chute - inflated by Eddie's hard work and dedication. Without Blair and Axel and Edgar and Eddie, Sid could not have helped Sara reproduce such a beautiful family. Take comfort in the knowledge that Sid's child, Suzy, and her children and her grandchildren have all now got a part of every one of you in them."

Despite the tears, everyone was, by now, beginning to be buoyant and happy, all eagerly talking of the role they had played in Sid's life.

"We all owe a huge debt of gratitude to Connor. He saved our lives at a time when he was the only one able to get round all the departments to cover us up and keep us warm when Sid got buried by the outsider's snow. Remember that time? Connor where are you? Stand up."

To thunderous applause Connor stood and bowed a mock bow, to everyone's amusement.

Brian gave them more to rejoice and pointed to each one of his subjects, in turn, as he talked about them. "Billy, you've kept Sid's big wrapping in good condition to protect us all and keep us together and warm, and Theola, you have worked with Tommy to keep us all comfortable. Both of you have cooled Sid down when he got too hot, thereby making life here, inside Sid, bearable. Daphne has commanded her defence force with determination, to fend off and destroy every one of Sid's evil bugs, and Wally has kept Sid's microphones nice and clean and shiny so that Lee, in listening, could hear everything she needed to hear and pass on to us from the outside."

Theola burst into tears, pride making her face light up. Her neighbouring tiny people put their arms around her to comfort her. Billy and Wally just beamed huge smiles and Daphne hid her face in embarrassment.

Brian looked over his army of tiny people with pride. He suddenly recognised an old friend.

"There you are, Max."

Max smiled and gave an embarrassed wave.

Brian smiled back and said, quietly, more to himself than to anyone in particular, "My friend Max, the mechanic…"

There was a pause as Brian remembered the times that he and Max had lazily passed the time of day chatting down in the kitchen, putting their world to rights and joking about some of the antics that the tiny people had got up to.

Brian shook his head and continued out loud, "How could I have almost forgotten my friend, Max? Without Max, Sid would never have walked, or lifted, or bent down to weed his garden, or hold his lovely Sara close to him. My friend Max - We have much to thank him for."

More thunderous applause.

"Look around you," Brian continued, his voice wavering under the emotion that he felt. Tears welled up in his eyes.

"Look at your neighbour. Some of you have never met before now, but you have all worked together, as a team, to make sure that Sid has been fit and well enough to enjoy his life outside. My team. What a team you are…Without any one of you, Sid would have found it extremely difficult to survive. You can all be proud of the work you have done, and you should all hold your heads up high in satisfaction of the good job that you have accomplished. You have all helped to make Sid a unique and amazing outsider. You have all enabled him to do the things that he did and achieve everything he wanted to achieve. I am proud to have been your leader…"

Sienna interrupted Brian's flow of uplifting words and held her hand up to quieten the things down.

When silence prevailed, she said, "There is one person that Brian has not mentioned here, today… That person is Brian, himself."

There was noisy cheering and clapping with Sienna's words.

"Brian has been a good leader. He has been strict when it was necessary, but he has always been fair. He has listened to our gripes, and he has provided many words of wisdom when we have needed them. He has always been there for us and I, for one, am glad that we had such a strong and knowledgeable leader to guide us and look after the servers."

Everyone was now euphoric, clapping their hands enthusiastically and cheering loudly.

Brian held his hands up in embarrassment, shaking his head. Tears of pride, and sadness, and joy all mixed up together, were wiped away by his coat sleeve.

When silence, once more, returned he decided that now was the time to prepare everyone for the inevitable.

With a trembling voice he said, "I want you all, now, to go to your beds and prepare yourselves for the big sleep. Don't be afraid of what is to come. I'm not. I'm looking forward to it and you should, too. We will all be together again soon, and I cannot wait to welcome you to a new life. A new life in a new Sid in a new world. Go, now, because I'm filling up again, and I want to remember you all as I see you now."

The tiny army turned and quietly queued for the exit doors, departing silently to go and lay down on their beds, eyes closed in anticipation of the big sleep. Some wept, others consoled them.

Brian and Sienna were the last to leave this room where everyone had always congregated. Pausing at the doorway, they turned to take one last look at the empty room.

Fondly embracing each other they kissed a last passionate kiss.

With a smile Sienna looked into Brian's eyes and said, "It's time…"

*

Outside, Sid felt a peace that he had never before experienced.

A peace that made him feel content with what he had achieved in his lifetime. He no longer heard the crying of his family. He knew that time heals and he smiled, inwardly, as he pictured them laughing and joking about the happy times that he had given them.

The remaining server in Brian's department shut down at one forty-five in the afternoon…

… And Sid died peacefully.